Paul pulled her down onto the bed

"I didn't mean this to happen," he muttered against her lips before his mouth closed on hers. The kiss was deep and probing as his hands moved over her....

Then suddenly he was on his feet and walking away. Kate pushed herself up and asked in confusion, "W-what's the matter?" Her voice was quavery.

He spun around and his face was dark. This was the old Paul, the one she thought had disappeared. "The matter is that I shouldn't have started this bloody stupid game at all." He looked keenly across the room at her. "You're a virgin, aren't you?"

Kate's head went up proudly. "Yes, I am. Is there anything wrong with that?"

Paul groaned. "Everything. Now get out, for both our sakes!"

MARJORIE LEWTY
is also the author of these

Harlequin Romances

and these

Harlequin Presents

Many of these titles are available at your local bookseller.

For a free catalogue listing all available Harlequin Romances
and Harlequin Presents, send your name and address to:

HARLEQUIN READER SERVICE,
M.P.O. Box 707, Niagara Falls, NY 14302
Canadian address: Stratford, Ontario N5A 6W2

Love Is a Dangerous Game

by

MARJORIE LEWTY

Harlequin Books

TORONTO • LONDON • LOS ANGELES • AMSTERDAM
SYDNEY • HAMBURG • PARIS • STOCKHOLM • ATHENS • TOKYO

Original hardcover edition published in 1980
by Mills & Boon Limited

ISBN 0-373-02421-5

Harlequin edition published August 1981

CHAPTER ONE

THE August heatwave had broken into thunder-storms and London was having a wet September. This morning, as Kate Reynolds picked her way along the streaming pavements of the City, past the towering buildings—old and new—where a great portion of the world's business took place, the sky was a uniform slate colour. Muddy water hissed under the wheels of the ceaseless procession of cars and vans and lorries, spewed across the road, carelessly splashing the hurrying pedestrians as it went, and finally gurgled in dismal rivulets down the grids.

Very appropriate, Kate thought with black humour, dragging the belt of her grey gaberdine mac tighter round her slim waist. Just the final touch to the last three days of unrelieved disaster.

She eased back the cuff of her wet mac to look once more at her watch and a trickle of rain ran down her arm, making her shiver, more with nerves than cold. Five to eleven. Zero hour approaching.

She stopped outside the imposing entrance to one of the great white tower blocks, her large, wide-set grey eyes fixed with something like panic on the bronze plate that said Barn Trekker Electronics Inc.

Why, for goodness' sake, should she go through this misery to try to get Jerry out of yet another scrape, even if it were the worst one of his scatty young life? Wouldn't she be justified in leaving him to cope on his own? He had to start taking responsibility for himself some day. Why not now?

But of course she knew why not. This last mess her young brother had got himself into would break Father's heart if he found out about it. Break his health too, finally. For a moment her throat choked up as she thought of the way he had been since last Sunday—insisting on carrying on his parish duties although he looked hardly fit to drag himself out of the house. She just *had* to make this interview a success somehow.

She blinked and swallowed, pushing back the wave of emotion. She had to keep a grip on herself so that she could present her arguments coolly and reasonably. She climbed the entrance steps and paused, out of the rain, to peer at her face in her small handbag mirror. Before she left home this morning she had taken particular trouble over her grooming, in the hope that nothing about her appearance should make a bad impression on this unknown, frightening individual she was going to see. This 'inhuman bastard', Jerry had called him.

But walking in the rain had played havoc with her careful efforts. The head-scarf which was supposed to be rainproof had long ago become soaked and was now tucked in a damp lump into her mac pocket. Her very fine, light-gold hair hung in darkened wet strands to her shoulders, enclosing a small, resolute face, out of which huge, clear grey eyes stared back at her. The light application of eye-shadow had smudged at one corner, finally marring the picture she wished to present of a quietly capable, reasonable young woman who would not easily be brushed aside.

She clicked her tongue in exasperation, dabbing at her eye with a handkerchief. Oh well, there was nothing she could do now about her appearance. She would have to try to make up for it by her demeanour—very cool and collected she would be. Not grovelling to ask a favour of this man, but rather appealing to his understanding and compassion. Jerry's description hadn't been encouraging, but Jerry had been under a strain when the man had interviewed him. A top man in a huge corporation like Barn Trekker must be able to judge people accurately, surely? He must have seen that Jerry wasn't really dishonest.

Somewhere in the distance a clock began to strike eleven with heavy strokes.

'Come on, then,' Kate said aloud, drawing in a shaky breath and lifting her rounded small chin. 'Let's get it over.'

The entrance lobby was vast and she felt as if she were dwindling as her heels clicked over green, flinty-hard tiles. But her secretarial experience gave her a certain confidence as she approached the imposing uniformed porter stationed behind a desk.

She drew herself up to her slim five feet four inches. 'I have an appointment with Mr Paul Caister, of Barn Trekker.'

The porter pointed to Kate's handbag and she opened it and held it out. Security precautions didn't surprise her any longer, as they had done when the family first moved to London from their quiet West Country village, six months ago.

The porter nodded and jerked his head towards a row of lifts. 'Top floor,' he said. 'You'll have to see Mr Caister's secretary.'

The top floor was so quiet that Kate felt she

should apologise to someone for the click of the lift gates as she closed them behind her. Wide carpeted corridors stretched to either side, punctuated by pale wood doors, each with its neat bronze plate. No clatter, no rush. This was evidently the nerve centre of the London branch of the Corporation, where the top brass operated.

'Look for a door on the left marked J. S. Bruce,' Jerry had told her this morning, his eyes glassy and his face flushed with fever. 'I suppose it's too much to hope that old Bruce himself will be back from the U.S.'

Yesterday afternoon, when he had come home pale and frightened, and blurted out the whole wretched story to her, Jerry had told her that James Bruce, the Personnel Director, was away in America. 'This Caister bloke's standing in for him, and he's an inhuman bastard. That's the whole trouble. Old Bruce would never have taken this hard line over a paltry thirty quid. He wouldn't have made me feel like a criminal.'

Kate almost said, 'But you *are* a criminal. Taking money that doesn't belong to you makes you a criminal, even if it is only thirty pounds and even if you can argue that you were only borrowing it until the end of the month.'

She hadn't said it. Jerry was 'family' and she had to try and help. She went over and closed the kitchen door in case Father should come out of his study, where he was supposed to be resting but was probably working on his sermon for next Sunday, or writing letters in the interest of one of the dozens of his parishioners who didn't seem able to cope with life in this tough North London parish he had been so eager to serve.

She leaned her back against the door and

looked over at her brother. 'And what's going to happen now?'

Jerry sprawled in his chair, a quiff of fair hair hanging over his forehead. He pushed it away and Kate saw the beads of sweat there. Jerry was having a bad scare this time. Perhaps it would take this to make him grow up at last.

'Oh, I'm bidden to wait upon his high and mightiness, Mr Paul Caister, tomorrow morning at eleven, to hear what sentence he's decided to pass on me.'

The show of bravado didn't convince Kate. 'You'll lose your job?'

'Lose my job? That's the least of it. The swine talked about prosecution!'

'Prosecution?' An icy wave passed through Kate's body. Police—magistrates' court—even prison! It was appalling, unthinkable. 'He can't do that!'

'I suppose he could, if he really wanted to be nasty.'

'But—but it would be too dreadful for Father. I think it would kill him—the disgrace——'

'Don't get worked up, Kate, for God's sake. I wouldn't have told you if I'd thought you were going to make such heavy weather of it.'

She glared at him angrily. 'Of course I'm worked up—how did you expect me to feel? You know what the doctor said on Sunday, after we got Father home—that he must take it easier and not worry so much about his work.'

She bit her lip hard as all the details of the scene in the vestry were suddenly, starkly vivid again. Her father's thin, rather frail body slumped in the chair, his face paper-white against the black of his cassock; his eyes closed and his hands working convulsively.

'He really is terribly tired, Jerry. Another attack like that one might—might——' She didn't dare to think of it. 'You must tell this Caister man tomorrow. Explain to him.'

'I did—this afternoon. He didn't want to know.'

'You told him about Father being ill, and what the shock might do to him—as a clergyman he'd probably think he had to resign his living, and that would just about finish him. *Did* you explain all that?'

'I didn't go into all the sob stuff,' said Jerry, sulky now. 'He's not the sort of bloke to be soft-soaped, Kate. You'd agree with me if you could see him, he's as hard as nails.'

Kate slumped into a chair and put a hand over her eyes. 'Oh Lord, Jay, what an idiot you are! Why did you have to get into this mess?'

There was a silence, then he said in an odd, strained voice, 'You don't think I meant to get into a mess, do you? I didn't think.'

That was the trouble with Jerry. It had always been, 'I didn't think.' She lifted her head wearily. 'You never——'

She didn't finish the sentence. Jerry was doubled up in his chair, sobbing like a little boy.

There was no point in trying to continue the discussion. Kate dropped back into the role of mother and comforter—the role she had played since their own mother died when she was ten and Jerry was six. Now, eleven years later, she felt that not much had changed. She got Jerry to bed, with an excuse of 'flu, for Father's benefit. By the time she went to bed herself the fever had become a reality and Jerry was running a high temperature—psychological, probably, but none the less real.

He had held on to her hand and stared up at her with swollen, red-rimmed eyes. 'What am I going to do, Kate? Oh God, what am I going to do?'

He was only seventeen and this was his first job. Kate gave him aspirins and sponged his hot cheeks. 'Go to sleep, dopey,' she told him. 'If you're not better in the morning I'll go and see the man myself.'

In the morning Jerry had been worse, and so now Kate was standing here, outside the door marked J. S. Bruce, with a hollow inside where her stomach should have been.

She took a deep breath, knocked, and went in.

The door opened into a narrow, windowless room, almost completely filled by a desk and a nest of steel filing cabinets. A secretary's office, of course, acting as a buffer between the man behind that inner door and the corridor outside.

A woman with untidy fair hair, and a harassed expression in pale blue eyes, looked up from the desk as Kate went in. 'Yes?' She frowned impatiently. 'What is it?'

Kate had her first words ready, the ones she had rehearsed and memorised. 'My name is Reynolds. I'm Jeremy Reynolds's sister. He was told to report here at eleven this morning, but he's ill and unable to come. As the matter was important I offered to come and see Mr Caister in his place.'

Pale eyes flicked over Kate's wet grey mac, which was clinging rather forlornly to her slim body, and the woman glanced down at a diary on the desk. 'There's no appointment marked here,' she snapped. 'I don't know anything about anyone called Reynolds.'

In a way that was a relief. Kate had had a horrid idea that everyone in the office must know about Jerry and what he had done. 'This *is* the Personnel Director's office? Mr Caister, acting for Mr Bruce?'

'Yes'—grudgingly—'but Mr Caister's extremely busy and I can't possibly disturb him. Your brother, whoever he is, had better come himself. And tell him to make a proper appointment.' The woman lowered her head to her typewriter in a gesture of dismissal.

Kate didn't move. 'I'm sorry to be a nuisance,' she said politely, 'but I'm afraid I must insist on your asking Mr Caister if he will see me.' Her eyes went to the closed inner door.

The secretary jumped to her feet, her cheeks showing spots of scarlet. '*Insist?* How dare you? I won't be dictated to, you know, I'm not here to be ordered about by any chit of a girl who cares to walk in and demand to be seen by one of the directors. What impudence!' She bridled, jerking her head back, her mouth closing like a trap.

Remembering her secretarial training, Kate could almost pity such hopeless inefficiency. This certainly wasn't the way to deal with callers who didn't have appointments. And anyway, she reminded herself, she *did* have an appointment. Well—sort of.

'I'll wait, then,' she said firmly, and sat down on a chair beside the filing cabinet.

Her action seemed to inflame the secretary. Her face was livid now, her pale blue eyes wild. 'You won't wait here, I'll not allow it. Of all the insolence—coming here and interrupting my work and badgering me! I'll ring for the porter to put you out. And you can tell your precious brother, whoever he is——'

Her voice rose to a screech and Kate realised that she was reacting out of all proportion to the situation. She must have been in a jittery state already, and any new demand on what poise she possessed must have been too much for her. She clutched Kate's arm, pulling her up from the chair. 'Get out! Go on, get out, before I——'

The door of the inner office burst open and a man's voice, deep and angry, said, 'What the hell's going on here? Miss Parkes, please explain why you have to use your office as a wrestling booth?'

He did not raise his voice, he was perfectly in control, but his presence chilled the atmosphere of the small office, like opening the lid of a deep-freeze cabinet.

The secretary shrivelled. She dropped Kate's arm and began to make little fluttering movements with her hands. 'Oh, Mr Caister, I'm so sorry, but this—this young person came in with some cock-and-bull story, demanding to see you, and she refused to leave, and I——' The pale blue eyes swam with tears.

The man didn't move, neither did his expression change. He stood, tall and dark and dangerous, towering over the wretched woman. 'Miss Parkes, I suggest that you take yourself out of this office until you're in a fit state to deal with your job. Go away and swallow some aspirins or black coffee or something and don't come back until you've got control of yourself.'

She made a despairing effort. 'I don't really need—— I'm quite all right, Mr Caister, it was just——' She lifted her eyes pleadingly to the implacable face of the man before her and choked into silence.

He stepped to the outer door and opened it. 'Out!' he ordered, and the unfortunate Miss Parkes scuttled away down the corridor.

He kept a hand on the door knob as he turned to Kate. 'Now,' he said, 'who are you and what do you want? Make it brief, please, I'm busy.' His eyes flicked over her without interest.

Kate was in no state to take in details of the man in front of her. She had an impression of height and leanness and hard muscular strength beneath the immaculately-cut business suit. He was younger than she had supposed—mid-thirties probably—and she saw exactly what Jerry had meant when he called Paul Caister an inhuman bastard. Her own instinct labelled him 'male chauvinist' in addition. Miss Parkes was hopelessly incompetent, but he shouldn't have treated a woman secretary like that, humiliating her before a stranger. It was cruel and unnecessary.

But she had to keep her cool somehow for Father's sake, she reminded herself. She had come to plead with this man for a favour, however much she hated him on sight.

She met the dark, angry eyes squarely. 'I'm Kate Reynolds, Jeremy Reynolds's sister. My brother had an appointment with you for eleven o'clock this morning, but he's not well enough to come himself, so I offered to see you in his place to—to find out what you've decided to do.'

An impatient frown had been settling between his straight dark brows while she was speaking. 'Reynolds? I don't know anyone called——' His expression changed, the straight, rather sensual mouth took a downward curve. 'Oh yes—Reynolds—the light-fingered young thug in Accounts who's been helping himself to the petty cash.'

There was such contempt in his tone that Kate almost gave up then and there. But somehow she managed to keep her voice even. 'If you could spare me just a minute or two, Mr Caister, I should be very grateful. There's something I'd like to explain to you.'

He hardly glanced at her as she stood there in her wet mac, her fair hair, darkened by the rain, hanging in limp strands round her small face, her eyelids slightly smudged.

'Two minutes,' he said. He turned and strode back into his office.

Kate followed him into a large, opulently-appointed room with wide windows that looked out at the sky and down at the City far below, dotted with ant-like traffic and divided by a narrow silver ribbon of river.

The man settled himself in a black leather executive chair behind a vast desk, his eyes on a file of papers, on which he had evidently been working. 'Sit down, Miss—er——'

'Reynolds,' said Kate. 'Thank you, but I'd rather stand. I won't keep you——'

'Sit *down*,' he repeated, with weary authority, not looking up.

Kate hesitated a moment and then sat down on the edge of the chair opposite him. It was galling to have to obey this hateful man, but she mustn't antagonise him, for Jerry's sake. Correction, she added mentally, for Father's sake.

Eventually he sat back in his chair, eyes narrowed under thick black lashes. 'Your brother's ill, you say. What's the matter with him?'

'I think it's 'flu. He's running a high temperature.'

'Oh yes?' The dark brows rose cynically. 'Very convenient! Quite a coincidence, in fact. So he sends his sister along to plead his cause. A girl might expect special treatment, was that the idea?'

It was going to be difficult to control her temper. 'No, Mr Caister, that was *not* the idea.' She spoke more forcefully than she had intended and there was a frosty sparkle in her wide grey eyes. 'And I haven't come to excuse my brother or plead his cause. There's no excuse for what he did. If it weren't for my father I'd have left Jerry to sort things out for himself. But my father's ill and I'm worried about him. He's a clergyman, and he's been overworking since we moved to London and the doctor says he must take it easy and avoid stress.' The words poured out now she had started. The man opposite had bent his head over his papers again and all she could see was the top of his head with its thick, springy black hair, but she rushed on, hoping he was listening. 'If Jerry was—if anything really bad happened to Jerry, I think it would—— I don't know what it would do to my father.'

In the silence that followed her outburst she felt as if her throat were held rigid by steel bands. Hadn't he heard what she had said? Wasn't he going to reply at all?

Moments dragged past until she was sure she would scream, and then at last he lifted his head and said, 'A touching story, but how do I know it's true? If your brother is a thief—which according to my information he certainly is—why shouldn't his sister be equally suspect?'

Kate stared at him, cold with shock. 'Do you believe I'm lying?'

The wide shoulders lifted in a faint shrug. 'Well, aren't you? The whole scenario looks suspiciously improbable to me. The ailing, elderly parent, the weak and erring brother, the noble self-sacrificing sister.' He smiled nastily. 'It's almost too good to be true.'

Kate stared at the heavy brass paperweight on the desk and itched to pick it up and hurl it at him. 'It *is* true, whether you believe it or not.'

He tapped long brown fingers on the desk impatiently. 'Well, supposing it is, what do you expect me to do about it?'

A flicker of hope arose. Eagerly she said, 'If—if you could give Jerry another chance? Perhaps in another department where there wouldn't be any loose money about so that he wouldn't—so that you could be sure——' she floundered helplessly for a moment, and then rushed on, 'or if you couldn't keep him on, at least let him repay the money, and—and—let the matter drop. Jerry's not really bad,' she urged. 'He's very young— only seventeen—and he's been in a few scrapes, as most boys have, but he's never done anything dishonest before. He only meant to borrow the money, he was going to put it back when he was paid next week.'

He said nothing and she had no idea whether she was getting through to him or not, but she had rehearsed what she would say and now she had started she had to see it through.

'It was just an impulse—taking the money—he didn't plan it or anything. You see, there was this girl and he wanted to take her out, to impress her.

He'd never been in love before and he got it very badly. He lost his head—you know how it is——'

The slam of Paul Caister's hand on the desk sounded like a pistol shot in the quiet office. 'That's enough, Miss Reynolds. I don't require the details of your brother's love life. You've had your two minutes, now you'd better go before I lose my patience.'

Kate caught her breath and her eyes went wide. What had she said to cause this reaction of fury in the man? Nothing, reason told her. He must have been in a vile temper when she came in—nothing to do with Jerry, obviously. That must be a very minor episode to him.

He got up from his chair and stood holding the door open for her to leave. 'But—but what will you do?' she faltered. She wasn't a timid girl, but it wasn't easy to confront this dark, angry man who towered above her, scowling. She got slowly to her feet, but she reached scarcely to his shoulder.

'Do? What the hell did you think I'd do? Did you imagine you could soften me up? Your precious brother would have done better to face up to coming himself instead of sending a decoy.'

'A—a decoy? I don't know what you mean.'

'Don't give me that line,' he sneered. 'How far would you have gone? Did you propose to offer yourself as a bed-partner in return for your brother's reprieve? What makes you think I'd be tempted?' His glance flicked over her slight body contemptuously.

She was breathing fast, but she managed to keep her head up as she glared at him, her hands gripping the back of the chair. 'That was your idea, Mr Caister, it wasn't mine. I'd have done anything else for you—worked for you, scrubbed floors for your wife—sewed, cooked—anything—anything at all. It's just a pity that, like all men, your thoughts seem to run exclusively on bed.'

There was no point in prolonging the interview. She had failed. Worse, she had probably made things even more desperate than they were already. She gathered every shred of her tattered dignity. 'Good morning, Mr Caister,' she said, and swept past him out of the office.

Once in the corridor her knees turned to jelly and she stumbled blindly to the lift. Mercifully it was still at the top floor. She fell into it and pressed the button, leaning against the side, shivering as the floor numbers passed in a blur before her eyes.

She hardly noticed when the lift stopped, and before she could pull herself together there was a soft shudder and it began to ascend again.

Kate panicked. There was no logical reason why it should be Paul Caister who had summoned the lift upwards, but somehow she knew it was. Her finger was already on the button when the lift sighed to a halt, but it was no use. The gates glided open and the man she had just left stood before her, almost filling the opening with his tall, formidable body.

He kept a restraining hand on the gate. 'We hadn't quite finished our discussion after all, Miss Reynolds,' he said smoothly.

She glanced antagonistically at him and quickly removed her gaze to the wall on the opposite side of the corridor. 'There's nothing to discuss.'

'I think there is,' he said crisply. He stepped into the lift beside her, clicked the gate shut and pressed the ground floor button. 'We'll continue our conversation off the premises.'

The lift was small and intimate, one of a slick fleet for personnel. Kate felt the breath leave her body as she was pressed against the hard, muscular shoulder of the man beside her.

He didn't appear to notice her embarrassment. As they swooped down he murmured, almost to himself, 'Besides, I can do without that idiot secretary woman breathing down my neck.'

The lift sighed to a stop. Paul Caister stepped out and gripped Kate's elbow firmly. 'Come along,' he ordered.

She saw the porter's eyes on them. 'Let me go!' she muttered, pulling away. 'I'm not your prisoner.'

Prisoner! That was an ill-chosen word. She had a sudden chilling picture of Jerry standing in a dock, flanked by policemen, and she stopped struggling.

'We're going for coffee, Baines,' Paul Caister called pleasantly across to the porter, and the man seemed to spring to attention. 'Back in half an hour. I'm expecting my sister. If she comes before I'm back ask her to wait, will you?'

'Right, sir.' The man saluted smartly and Kate found herself led out again into the wet street, and round the corner to a coffee-house in a small, ancient-looking building tucked away deep in the heart of the old city. The low-ceilinged room was dark with heavy carved wood and hazy with smoke. The aroma of expensive coffee floated around, as it must have done here for a couple of hundred years.

They sat on high-backed seats upholstered in burgundy velvet, in an enclosed alcove. 'It's quiet and civilised here,' Paul Caister said, glancing round the half-empty room. 'We can talk.'

Kate looked at the hard face of the man sitting opposite. It was a strikingly handsome face; dark and brooding, the near-black liquid eyes giving it a slightly foreign look. He was regarding her narrowly and his long lashes lowered towards high cheekbones made his face hollow-cheeked, hungry-looking. His mouth looked somehow hungry too—or was it merely bad-tempered?—the lips thin and straight, the faintest movement making them cynical. It was a sensual mouth too; Kate was quite experienced enough to recognise that fact.

She frowned, suddenly confused to realise she had been staring at him. 'I don't understand. Not five minutes ago you nearly threw me out of your office.'

'That was five minutes ago. The situation has changed.' He leaned back, relaxed, very self-assured. 'You made me an offer. You said you'd do anything for me—or for my wife—if I'd get your brother off the hook.'

An elderly waiter approached. 'Coffee, please, Henry. How goes it with you?' Paul Caister's voice was friendly as he spoke to the old man.

The waiter beamed. 'Nicely, thank you, sir. You back for long, Mr Caister? How was the weather in Hong Kong?'

'Delightful—London could learn a thing or two.' He glanced at the deep, lead-lighted window where the rain cascaded down outside.

The waiter padded off and returned almost immediately with a tray of coffee. Paul Caister picked up the pot. '*Is* the offer still open?' he repeated. 'Cream? Sugar?'

'No, thank you.' Kate needed her coffee very black and strong. She sipped the rich dark liquid and felt the stimulating heat racing through her gratefully, giving her courage to meet the hard look of the man opposite.

'I don't happen to have a wife,' he continued, helping himself to cream, 'but there's something you might do for me as a quid pro quo.'

Kate hesitated. Then she saw again her Father's chalk-white face when they brought him home on Sunday, after his collapse in church when evening service was over. 'Yes,' she said steadily, 'the offer's still open.'

'With certain exceptions, of course, which you mentioned?' The long, thin mouth twisted sardonically.

She nodded in silence, disliking the man more every minute. She almost preferred him when he was blisteringly angry.

'I'll keep that in mind,' he drawled. 'But actually my proposition doesn't include bed.' The dark eyes glittered briefly. 'It isn't immoral. Or illegal. Or—to complete the quote—fattening.' He glanced dismissively at that part of her body that was visible above the table and added, 'though I don't imagine you need to worry on that score. Won't you slip your coat off? It's warm in here.'

She drew into her grey mac as if it were armour, defending her against this hateful man who seemed to enjoy humiliating her. 'No, thank you,' she said stiffly.

He stirred his coffee, looking down thoughtfully into his cup. Kate watched the long, brown fingers moving with precision. She wouldn't have thought he would take cream in his coffee; it seemed out of character.

He drank deeply and appreciatively, then put down the cup and said, 'Now—to business. I'm returning to Hong Kong tomorrow to finish off a job there. I'll be away about a month, returning to England late in October. For various reasons it would suit me to have my fiancée join me there and stay on until I leave.' He was silent for a moment and then shot at her, 'Is that practicable, do you think?'

Kate lifted puzzled eyebrows. Why shouldn't he take his fiancée to Hong Kong? Poor girl, she added mentally, pitying anyone engaged to this man. 'Yes, why not?' she said.

'Good. You agree, then, we can get down to details.'

'I don't quite understand. What do you want *me* to do—make arrangements for your fiancée? Bookings or something?'

He moved his shoulders impatiently. 'My dear girl, use your head. I want you to *be* my fiancée for a month or so, while I'm in Hong Kong. Look on it as a job, if you like. I don't know what job you do, but I'd pay you twice what you're getting at present. You'd have a free holiday— Hong Kong's delightful just now—and a new wardrobe of suitable clothes.' His eyes passed with distaste over the damp grey mac.

Kate choked a little. 'You're mad! I couldn't— couldn't pretend——'

'That we were in love with each other? Oh, I expect I could convince 'em.' He looked disgustingly complacent. 'Once they got over the shock, my friends would probably decide that I'm the type of man to fall for a nice little clergyman's daughter. The improbable always intrigues people where love—whatever that is—is concerned, haven't you noticed? Can't you hear them? "I don't know *what* he saw in her!" he mimicked nastily. 'But they'll accept it. They'll have to,' he added, tossing down the remainder of his coffee.

'So you *do* believe I'm a clergyman's daughter now, do you?' said Kate, more to gain time than because his opinion was important.

'Oh yes, I've decided that you were telling the truth. Your exit line when you left my office was entirely convincing and in character. That was what put this plan of mine into my head. Contrary to your sweeping indictment of my sex, I don't happen to be looking for a girl to sleep with just at the moment. I need to concentrate exclusively on my business problems.'

Kate could hardly believe her own ears. Of all the arrogant, conceited, overbearing—words failed as resentment flared into fury. But she couldn't afford to give vent to her feelings—not yet. Not until she was convinced that she had failed completely in her attempt to protect Father from the results of Jerry's idiocy. She had to stall, to give herself time to think.

'It was very sudden, wasn't it? This brilliant idea of yours?' She couldn't help her lip curling with distaste.

'All the best ideas are sudden. It came to me the instant you said, with such heartrending emotion, "I'll do anything for you—anything at all——" I thought that if you were sincere, if you weren't play-acting, it would solve my problems.'

The first shock was wearing off now and all that remained was cold disgust. 'And what about *my* problems?'

He brushed that aside. 'What problems? You're not married, are you?' He managed to make it sound insultingly improbable.

'No.'

'Well, surely anything else can be coped with.' He shot her a keen look. 'Is there a man in the offing? Someone who would put up resistance?'

Before they moved to London there had been quite a queue of men in the offing. None of them had been special, though, and in the past six months she had avoided making any relationships that would put a demand on her time. There had been so much to do: getting the large, inconvenient vicarage more or less straight; helping Father with all the small chores that a vicar's wife is expected to do, if he has one. Most evenings were spent working on her languages and attending classes. One day Kate Reynolds was going to command a top secretarial job.

'I'm a career girl,' she said coldly. 'I don't ask any man's permission.'

'Spoken like a truly liberated woman!' He smiled nastily.

Too late she realised what her words implied and to her intense horror she felt the blood rushing into her face. 'I'm not a liberated woman, not in the way you imply,' she said quickly.

He sighed. 'My dear good girl, don't let's get involved with *that* subject again. I assure you I wasn't implying anything in particular, so let's get off the subject of bed once and for all, shall we? I promise you nothing is further from my mind. You don't fancy me—I don't fancy you. Is that quite clear?' He paused to let that sink in and then said, 'Now, what do you say to my proposal?'

In the dim, smoky atmosphere of the coffee room his eyes glittered darkly. It was quite unreasonable, but Kate felt a strong prick of fear inside her, a warning of something unknown and shattering. 'I—I couldn't,' she stammered. 'It's too ridiculous to think about.'

The dark brows went up. 'I warn you, Miss Reynolds, you'd better begin thinking about it. Because if not——'

She gasped. 'You mean—if I won't do this crazy thing you're asking you'll take it out on Jerry?'

His lips thinned. 'Your brother has already taken it out on himself. All I should do would be to allow justice to take its course.'

The words ran through her like a trickle of ice. She had been in a magistrates' court once, giving evidence about a motoring offence she had witnessed, and the memory of how the wretched defendant had looked when caught in the clutches of the law still had the power to make her shiver. And Jerry's case would be much, much worse.

Paul Caister stood up. 'I must get back to the office now. I'll leave you here to finish your coffee and make up your mind. If you decide to go along with my suggestion, come and tell me and we'll take it from there. If you don't return I'll know what to think—and what to do,' he added laconically.

Kate sat frozen, watching the man's tall, broad back as he walked out of the room. The window beside the table overlooked the steps outside and through the misty glass she saw him again, running up agilely, apparently unconscious of the rain. The supreme egoist—even the weather would have no power to turn him from his course.

It took that thought to persuade her finally that if she didn't fall in with his outrageous plan he would do exactly what he said, with all the horrible unthinkable consequences.

She emptied the last of the black coffee into her cup and drank off the now tepid liquid. There was really no choice, was there? She had to agree. The prospect of having to arrange details confused and appalled her. A man could brush aside domestic matters, but a woman couldn't. That was the difference still.

She put a hand to her hot forehead, willing herself to be calm. She must hang on to her priorities, and her first priority was Father's health. Everything came back to that.

All right, Mr Paul Caister, she muttered between her teeth. I'll be your fiancée for a month, if that's your price.

Having made the decision, doubts began to recede. Out in the streets the giant buildings didn't seem so overpowering, or herself so tiny and insignificant. The rain was stopping and there was even a watery sun trying to break through.

It would all be good experience, she told herself. When she finally applied for her top secretarial job she could mention casually that she had worked in the Far East. That would sound good. She was actually smiling faintly as she went up in the lift again to the top floor.

The luckless secretary had not come back yet and the outer office, when Kate knocked and went in, was empty. The door to the inner sanctum was ajar and voices came from inside.

A female voice, light and amused, said, 'You're

not contemplating marrying the girl, then, Paul?'

'*Marry* her?' The sound of the deep, disdainful voice sent a shiver of awareness through Kate and again she was acutely conscious that he held the future of her small family in his unfeeling grasp. 'Have a heart, Polly! Marriage is out for me in the foreseeable future. And, apart from that, can you see me marrying a little grey mouse of a clergyman's daughter?'

A light laugh. 'Not exactly, Paul dear. But are you quite sure about her? Not all clergymen's daughters are little grey mice, you know.'

'This one is,' he said grimly. 'Wait until you see her.'

'You're quite sure she'll come back?'

'Oh, she'll come back. If her story was true and she really has got her aged parent's good at heart, then she's got no choice, has she?'

Kate's fingernails bit into the palms of her hands. Insulting, arrogant *pig*!

'But what if the girl really falls for you? Have you thought of that?'

'I can deal with that if and when it happens. But naturally I'll take good care to see that it doesn't.'

The woman laughed again. 'If you weren't my brother I could slay you for that, Paul. You really are the limit!'

Kate didn't wait to hear any more. If she got any angrier she would rush into the office and throw something at this impossible man—either that or dash away quickly and take a bus home, her mission having failed. Either course was an admission of defeat, and Kate had reached the stage where she wasn't going to admit defeat. She was going to get her own back on Mr Paul Caister if it was the last thing she did. Every word he uttered stiffened her resolution.

Pulling herself up very straight and tightening the belt of her grey gabardine mac, she pushed open the office door wide, without knocking. There was the light of battle in her clear grey eyes.

'Here's the little grey church mouse, Mr Caister—Paul,' she smiled brilliantly. 'Come scurrying back to pick up the crumbs that fall from your table.'

Without waiting to be asked she sat down and straightened her mac over her knees. 'Now,' she said pleasantly, 'shall we get on with the briefing?'

CHAPTER TWO

Two pairs of dark eyes were turned towards Kate, the man's arrogant and sardonic, the woman's dancing with mischief.

'There you are, Paul, I warned you, didn't I? The little grey mouse can speak up for herself.' She lifted a hand towards Kate. 'I'm Polly Chard, this crazy man's sister. All right, Paul, you needn't scowl like that. You *are* crazy, you know you are, setting up a game like this.'

She was draped elegantly over a small chair near the window. In fact, Kate saw at a glance, elegance was the word for this young woman, from her slim kid shoes to the expertly-fashioned urchin cut of her gleaming black hair. She wore a suit of pale amethyst velvet, with an enormous silver and amethyst brooch, in the shape of a flying bird, pinned to the lapel. A short fur coat was tossed across the chair beside her. She looked much younger than her brother.

'And you're Kate?' she enquired. A quick turn of her head. 'You did say Kate, didn't you, Paul?'

Her brother was leaning against the window-frame near her, arms folded, an expression of brooding irritation on his dark, handsome face.

'Yes,' he said shortly.

His sister pulled a face at him and looked back towards Kate. 'And you're going along with this ridiculous game that Paul's been telling me about?'

Kate folded her hands together on her lap, pleased with her self-control. 'I haven't any choice, it seems. And as your brother points out, it will be a pleasant holiday for me,' she added calmly.

Polly chuckled. 'I wouldn't bet on being engaged to Paul turning out all fun and games!'

Her brother made an impatient movement of his broad shoulders. 'Cut it out, Polly, you know the score. It's not a joke.'

She stood up and laid a hand on his coat sleeve. 'No, sweetie, I know, I know. Never mind, dear, I'm sure Kate will help you out splendidly.' She threw a wicked grin at Kate.

Kate felt rather than saw the man's eyes on her. Furiously she thought that he might have been examining some clapped-out jalopy, and was still not convinced that the engine would start. 'We'll just have to hope so,' he said.

He moved restlessly to the desk and picked up a letter, frowning over it, quite obviously a man itching to get back to the really important things in life, disturbed and irritated by feminine chatter.

'I've got a lot to get through today, Polly. I'm determined to leave everything straight for Bruce when he gets back.' He tossed the letter on to the desk with a grunt of frustration and gave all his attention to his sister. 'I'll have to leave everything to you, to do the best you can. Get this girl out to me in Hong Kong as soon as possible. Phone me when you fix what flight she's coming on. And many thanks,' he added as an afterthought.

His sister raised smooth dark brows and lifted

one hand, rubbing the thumb and forefinger together meaningly.

'Oh lord, yes, I'd forgotten.' Paul yanked a cheque book from his pocket, scribbled on a cheque and tore it out, all in one impetuous movement. 'That cover it?'

Polly looked at it. 'I'd imagine so. I'll ask your agent to book a flight and charge it to your account, shall I?' She folded the cheque and placed it in her black kid handbag. 'I'll let you know if we spend any more.'

She picked up her fur jacket and slung it round her shoulders. 'Come along then, Kate. We'll leave this man to be a captain of industry. He loves it.' She moved to the door and a waft of expensive perfume moved delicately with her.

Kate glanced uncertainly at the top of the man's bent head; the angle of that shining, well-groomed head of dark hair seemed in itself a contemptuous dismissal. 'Goodbye, Mr Caister,' she said stiffly.

He glanced up briefly, not meeting her eyes. 'Goodbye, Miss—er—Kate.' He turned back to the desk.

The sound of her name on his lips stirred something deep and hotly chaotic inside her. How on earth was she going to manage to pretend, even for a month, that she was in love with this man, who managed to arouse such intense hostility in her? She just couldn't imagine.

Down in the entrance hall Polly shrugged her arms into her fur jacket and said, 'I'm going to pick up a cab to take me to the West End—I've got a hair appointment. Can I drop you anywhere?'

'Thanks, but I'm going the other way. I'll get

a tube from Liverpool Street, we're not far from there.'

Polly nodded. 'Okay, if you're sure. Well now, look, we must arrange to meet. I think you'd better come to my place tomorrow morning.' She opened her bag and handed Kate a card. 'I open the shop at half past nine, so perhaps you could be there around nine? Could you manage that?'

Kate nodded dumbly. She was beyond wondering what she could or could not manage. All she wanted now was to be alone to face all the details and snags that kept thrusting themselves to the surface of her mind.

'Super, I'll see you then and we'll make plans. 'Bye for now.' Polly smiled her urchin smile and tripped off across the tiled hall, moving gracefully, like a model.

Kate watched her go. Polly Chard lived in a world of glamour and fashion that was as different from her own world as it could possibly be. But at least she seemed warm and inclined to be friendly—which was more than could be said for her brother. You couldn't help liking Polly.

As she went out into the cold drizzle of the autumn day she thought that that was the one bright spot in this nightmare of a morning.

When Kate arrived home an hour later she found Jerry sprawling in a chair beside the kitchen fire. He looked white and haggard, but he jumped to his feet smartly the moment she came into the room.

'Don't say anything, Sis, I can guess how it went. I want to talk to you first. Come and sit down.'

She glanced round the big, old-fashioned kitchen. 'Where's Father? Is he all right?' Before she left home this morning she had dreamed up the idea of telling Father she was going to apply for a job. She had been halfheartedly applying for jobs since they moved, and it had become more and more obvious recently that she would have to earn some money soon, but the difficulties of being away from the house all day had loomed larger in her mind than the financial situation, so far.

Jerry grabbed her arm impatiently. 'Yes, he's okay. He went out to see some woman who's been taken to hospital.'

He urged her into a chair by the fire, sank into the one opposite and leaned forward eagerly.

'Kate, I've been doing a lot of thinking since you went out this morning. I shouldn't have let you go. I've been feeling an absolute heel for letting you in for it. It was my own stupid fault and I should have faced up to it.' He studied her face anxiously. 'Was it very bad?'

She gave him a wary look. Jerry had been penitent before and it hadn't lasted. The trouble over absenteeism at school—the period, later on, when Father found out that he was spending most of his time with some other students in the wine bar instead of attending lectures—that awful business when the Head of the college contacted all parents about drug-taking (fortunately Jerry had decided that once was enough). It all came back to her now.

'It wasn't a very pleasant interview,' she admitted.

He nodded unhappily. 'That brute Caister didn't want to know, I suppose?'

The hard, dark face of Paul Caister seemed to float in front of her eyes. 'Not really,' she said.

For some reason she didn't want to discuss Paul Caister with Jerry.

'Is he—did he say——?'

'We had a talk,' Kate told him carefully. 'I explained about Father. He didn't come to any conclusion then and there, but I think he'll consider it again before he—before he does anything definite.'

Jerry's eyes searched hers anxiously. 'But what did you *think*, Kate? You must have got some idea whether he was going to——' he swallowed'—to put me in the dock.'

She shook her head. 'I don't know, Jerry. I really don't know whether I got through to him or not.' She glanced quickly at him. 'Have you told Father anything about all this? Do you think he's guessed you were in trouble again?'

'No, I haven't told him a word and I don't think he's guessed. He looked into my room this morning to see how I was and if I wanted anything. I told him you'd brought me some breakfast and that I was much better and was going to get up. I said that I'd be going back to work tomorrow. That was a whopper, in a good cause.'

He stood up and walked restlessly over to the table, thumping his fist down on it. 'God, what a fool I've been! That was a good job I had. Barn Trekker is a top company. I might, in time, have got transferred to the technical side—working with my hands. I'd like that better, I could have got really interested in it. But I suppose I've mucked up my chances now.'

Kate thought he looked really angry with himself, not sorry for himself as he had done before when things had gone wrong. He wasn't trying to put the blame anywhere but where it belonged, either. Perhaps Jerry really was growing up at last. Perhaps if he got another chance he would make the most of it.

'Do you think I ought to tell Dad?' he said. 'Break it to him so that it wouldn't be an awful shock if the worst happens? I will, Kate, if you say so. It would be awful for him if—if they came and—and took me away all of a sudden.'

Kate's mouth softened. Jerry really was thinking of someone else besides himself this time. 'Don't say anything yet,' she told him. 'Wait until I've seen him. I want to find out how he is. He shouldn't——'

She paused, lifting her head at the sound of steps in the passage outside. A moment later the kitchen door opened and Father stood there, smiling at them both, a tall thin man in a tweed suit, greying, stooped slightly. His clerical collar stood away from his neck, which seemed to Kate to have shrunk lately. He looks—fragile, she thought, with a quick pang.

'I met the postman,' he said. He dropped two unopened envelopes on the table and came and stood in front of the fire, rubbing his hands together and holding them out to the warmth.

'Couldn't find my gloves,' he explained. 'Had to go out to the hospital urgently—old Mrs Warren from up the road—fell from a chair, trying to put a new bulb in the light.' He shook his head worriedly. 'She shouldn't be living alone, she's nearly eighty. It's not right.'

'Hasn't she got anybody?' Kate asked, although she could guess the answer. Old Mrs Warren was only one of the many lonely people to whom her father gave his care and assistance so unstintingly.

'Apparently not.' He gazed into the fire in silence for a moment. 'You know, I believe she was almost glad it had happened. With a broken hip she'll be in hospital, fed and warm and comfortable for a while. I really must see what can be done to make life more tolerable for her when she comes out of hospital—if she comes out.'

He stretched his hands, putting one on Jerry's shoulder, one on Kate's. 'How lucky I am to have a family, two such grand children. I count my blessings every day.'

Kate patted the hand that lay on her shoulder. It was cold and the knuckles protruded bonily. She felt a surge of compassion, facing the fact that Father was getting old. He had already been middle-aged when he married their mother, and this year he would be sixty-five. Retiring age. But she couldn't imagine Father retiring; he would work himself into the—— She bit her lip, appalled at the direction her thoughts were taking.

I must look after him, she vowed, because he'll never look after himself. His work confronted him with all the cruelties and sorrows of the world and yet he had remained curiously unworldly.

Sometimes she thought he was a saint.

She said quickly, 'I've made some of your favourite potato and onion soup for lunch.' She got up and went over to the cooker. 'Would you like me to bring it to your study and then you can have a rest on the couch? It'll be nice and warm in there, I lit the stove before I went out.'

'Thank you, my dear, that would be splendid.' He looked down at Jerry. 'You're really feeling better, my boy? You had a nasty turn, you mustn't hurry back to work.'

'No, Dad,' Jerry mumbled, hunching his shoulders as if to ward off something vague and threatening.

'And you, Kate——' Francis Reynolds turned to his daughter '——did you get very wet? It turned out an atrocious morning. How did your interview go, do you think? I want to hear all about it.'

Kate lifted a pan on to the cooker and picked up a long spoon. 'Quite promising, I think. I'll tell you when I bring your soup in.'

Her father pulled a face. 'That means I'm in the cook's way. Very well, my dear, I'll take myself off and read my letters.'

As the door closed Jerry got up and moved restlessly across the room to the window. 'God, this is awful! He looked tired, Kate, didn't you think? What am I going to do?'

She lit the gas under the pan of soup. 'Leave it, Jerry,' she said abruptly. 'There's nothing you *can* do.'

She heard again Paul Caister's deep, disdainful voice saying, 'Your brother's already taken it out on himself,' and she felt her stomach contract.

He spun round and faced her. 'Look, Kate, I can't stick this doing nothing, not knowing—I'm going to tell Dad about it all.'

'No!' She flung down the spoon and it fell with a clatter to the tiled floor. She clutched his arm as he stumbled past her. 'No, Jerry, you mustn't. I—I've got an idea.'

He stopped instantly, staring at her wildly, the blood staining his pale cheeks. 'There's something you haven't told me, Kate. Is there a hope? Did Caister say something? Suggest some way out?'

Clicking her tongue impatiently she picked up the spoon and washed it under the tap. 'Look, Jerry, there just *may* be a way out. But I can't tell you until I've talked to Father. You'll just have to wait. But if you go and blurt it out to him you'll spoil everything. Now, go and sit down and shut up.'

He hesitated, seemed about to say something and then thought better of it and shuffled to his chair. In a tense silence Kate set a tray with bread and fruit and went back to stir the soup.

Her mind was weary with the obstacles she had been turning over and over on her way home; practical obstacles that loomed larger and larger the more she thought about them.

It was all very well for Paul Caister to shrug off her problems with a lordly, masculine, 'What problems?' There were plenty. If she went off for a month who would look after the house? Who would clean and cook and shop? Who would do the washing and ironing? Who would attend to the paraffin stoves they relied on for heat in the old-fashioned house in all the rooms except the kitchen? Who would make sure, tactfully, that Father was not overdoing things and was getting enough to eat?

The neighbours—one or two of them—would probably pop in now and then, but that wouldn't be enough, not in the present circumstances.

In the study she found her father sitting beside the stove in his shabby, much-loved leather chair. He was surrounded, as usual, by his books and he held a letter in his hand. He smiled at her as she set the tray down beside him. 'That soup smells delicious. Come and talk to me while I have my lunch—or are you ready for yours?'

'Not yet.' She dropped to the rug at his feet and watched him sip the hot soup appreciatively. He was better, she thought, with a wave of relief. He must be—this was the first time he had shown any enthusiasm for food since his collapse last Sunday.

Her load of worry lightened a little. But even so, could she safely leave him for a month to cope on his own? And if she didn't accept Paul Caister's terms, could Father stand the stress of what might happen to Jerry? She felt as if she were being stretched painfully in two directions at once.

He put down his spoon. 'Now, tell me about your interview. Any good?' He had been encouraging her to look for a job. She was wasting her talents and her training woefully, he said.

'Could be,' she said carefully. She twiddled a strand of the wool rug between her finger and thumb. 'But I'm afraid it's not really on. They would want me to go abroad for a month, almost immediately.'

'Abroad? Where?'

She shrugged, dismissing the idea. 'The other side of the world—Hong Kong.' She watched her father's expression; if he showed dismay or alarm for any reason whatever she would tell the Caister man she had changed her mind. Perhaps he wouldn't be vindictive enough to keep his threat about Jerry. She'd just have to risk it.

Her father leaned back in his chair and she could find nothing but pleasure and gratification in his face. 'Well now, that sounds absolutely splendid. You must have made quite an impression, my dear, to get an offer like that. You'll accept, of course. Young people shouldn't miss the opportunity to travel, these days. And you'd enjoy it, wouldn't you?'

She looked down at her hands. 'I suppose it would be a good experience.'

Her father's eyes were twinkling as she lifted her own eyes to meet them and she thought that for a simple man he was amazingly perceptive. 'But you consider I'm not capable of looking after myself while you're away, is that it?'

She grimaced helplessly. 'Well, darling, *are* you?'

'Maybe not. But then, you see, the matter might not arise.' He handed her a letter. 'Read that and then tell me if you can doubt that God moves in a mysterious way.' He chuckled.

Kate unfolded the sheet and recognised the firm, no-nonsense handwriting of her Aunt Ella. Aunt Ella was her father's younger sister and lived alone in a cottage in Westmorland. Since Uncle Tom's death, two years ago, it had been suggested once or twice that she should move south to be nearer her brother and his family, but nothing had come of it. She was, she argued, too settled in her ways to uproot herself and she loved her cottage. She had disapproved strongly of her brother's move to take up a living in London. She could *not* understand, she had written, how anyone could choose to live in such a godforsaken place as London, and had added with her own brand of dry humour that she supposed that was why Francis had chosen to move—so that he could take God with him.

Now she wrote, 'My dear Francis, This will no doubt amaze you. I'm asking to be allowed to come and visit you for a few weeks. It seems that

the floods we've had up here this month have
done terrible things to my poor old cottage and it
has to have one wall entirely rebuilt if it's not to
fall around my elderly ears. As I don't fancy the
prospect of living under tarpaulin at this time of
year (which is, apparently, what it would amount
to) I'm begging your hospitality. I would insist
upon paying my way and working my passage as
well, and if Kate has qualms about an interfering
busybody of an aunt, then it might be an opportunity for her to take an outside job. You tell
me she's been too busy since you moved to look
for one, but I'm sure that by now she would be
quite glad to exchange the kitchen sink for a typewriter, clever girl that she is. Well now, brother
dear, let me know if you can put up with me. I
should so enjoy being with you all again and for
that pleasure would even tolerate the horrors of
the great metropolis. Your affectionate sister,
Ella.'

She looked up to see the gladness in her
father's face. 'Isn't it splendid, Kate? Couldn't be
better, or more timely. Oh, it will be so good to
see Ella again. And there's another thing——' He
put on his glasses and searched among the papers
on the table beside him. 'Yes, here it is. An
epistle from the Bishop. His Grace is somewhat
surprisingly considering the possibility of giving
me some help here. He has a young man in mind
who's anxious to take Holy Orders but wants to
be sure he's fitted for the practical side of the
work, which is very sensible of him, so he'd like
to do a year on the beat, so to speak, before going
into theological college. The bishop asks for my
thoughts on the subject.'

He put down the important-looking missive

and beamed at her. 'So you see, Kate, blessings abound on my unworthy head.'

'Rubbish,' said Kate. 'The Bishop jolly well knows what you're worth here. He wants to make sure you don't wear yourself out.'

It *was* good, she assured herself. But everything was working one way, and that way was to close all avenues of escape from her promise to Paul Caister.

'So now,' said her father, putting a hand gently on her shoulder, 'you can set out on your travels with an easy mind. You'll let them know that you accept the job?'

'Yes,' said Kate slowly. 'Yes, I suppose there's nothing to stop me going now.'

Back in the kitchen she found Jerry prowling about like a caged animal.

'Well?' He looked round abruptly and stood stock still. She saw that his fingers were clenched into his palms, but he tried to grin. 'What's the verdict of the court? Life or death?'

'Sit down and have your lunch and I'll tell you.' She went over to the cooker.

The easiest way was to tell Jerry the precise facts, and that was what she did. He stared at her, open-mouthed. 'Engaged to Caister? You're *not*, Kate! You couldn't marry a man like that.'

'Of course not,' she said crossly. 'It's only a sham—a pretence—something he dreamed up for reasons of his own. Don't ask me what they are, he didn't confide in me.' Her lip curled a little.

'But why——'

'Oh, Jerry, be your age,' she told him impatiently. 'I've told you what happened. I went to ask him for leniency for you, for Father's sake. He didn't go much for that argument, but finally he offered me a bargain. He would let you off if I'd agree to act as his fiancée for a month, while he was in Hong Kong. And *act* is the operative word.'

'And you agreed? Oh, Kate, thank you, you're the absolute tops!' Jerry's spirits began to revive miraculously. 'Hong Kong, that'll be fabulous!'

'I hope so,' she said shortly.

'But it *will*. And you'll cope all right, you always cope, and it's only for a month.' He regarded her with a touch of anxiety. 'You don't mind too much, do you? I mean, it'll be good experience for you, going abroad, won't it? You've always wanted to travel, and——'

She plonked a bowl of soup in front of him. 'All right, Jerry, let's leave it. I've agreed and that's that. Aunt Ella will be coming from Keswick to look after things here while I'm away.'

Jerry nodded. 'Okay, Kate.' He looked slightly chastened. 'Does Father know?'

'Only that I've had the offer of a job in Hong Kong for a month. And that's all he *must* know. Understood?'

'You bet,' her brother promised fervently. 'Oh gosh, I feel as if I'd been given a new life. I'll make the best of it, Kate, you'll see.'

She watched him as he made short work of his bowl of soup and her eyes softened. He looked so young in his shabby jeans and skinny tee-shirt, she could hardly believe that only three and a half years separated them.

'Mind you do,' she said.

It came as no surprise to Kate, next morning, to find that the 'shop' that Polly had mentioned was a boutique—very small, just a sliver of plate glass window wedged between a jeweller's on one side and a bespoke tailor's on the other—and very elegant. It was situated at the extreme edge of Mayfair.

The window displayed one exquisite gown, a swirling confection of honey-gold chiffon, the camisole top composed of a myriad tiny pleats, the skirt foaming out against the background drape of rich bitter-chocolate velvet. Beside it lay one perfect golden orchid. That was Polly's touch, Kate thought admiringly, she had a flair for clothes—beautiful, sophisticated clothes like the ones she wore herself, not the trendy variety.

She caught a glimpse of herself in the jeweller's window and saw a slim girl, neat and ordinary-looking in a short grey coat over a pleated skirt and pink sweater. At least she didn't look like a drowned rat today—or rather a drowned grey mouse. But she wasn't in Polly Chard's league— or in her brother's league either.

Still, she wasn't setting out to impress him. He had seen her at her worst yesterday, and if he still wanted her for this scheme of his, that was his business, not hers.

She hadn't slept much last night, and in the small hours she had decided on her future attitude towards Paul Caister. She would be cool, calm and completely unemotional. Yesterday she had let him get under her skin, with his arrogant, contemptuous treatment of her. He wouldn't do it again, she promised herself. She knew the kind of man he was now, and she would think of him merely as a particularly dislikeable boss. She would work for him and do as she was told for a month and then it would be over. Meanwhile she would make the most of the opportunity for travel, knowing that it would help her to get a good job later on.

Buoyed up by this sensible resolution, she pressed the bell on the yellow-painted door next to the shop entrance, and waited.

A disembodied voice said tinnily, 'Yes, who is that, please?'

Kate announced herself and Polly said, 'Oh yes, of course—hullo, Kate. Come straight up, the door's open.'

Kate climbed a narrow, rather dark staircase, to find Polly waiting at the top in an immaculate black suit with a thick twisted rope of tiny pearls at her throat. She looked stunning.

'Come on in, Kate,' she said, taking her arm. 'You're just in time to say goodbye to Paul, he's leaving in a minute or two.'

Kate's inside shook. She hadn't expected him to be here this morning and her good resolutions hadn't quite had time to jell.

'Here she is, Paul. Here's your dear little grey mouse,' Polly announced with a gurgle of laughter, and went to the far end of the long narrow room where a coffee percolator was sending out a delicious aroma.

Kate walked forward, vaguely aware of the colours and textures and general air of modern luxury that stamped the room with Polly's own individuality. But the only thing that really registered was the form of the tall, broad man standing in the window, replacing the telephone on its cradle.

The pale morning sunlight poured in, putting a gloss on his smooth dark hair, emphasising the brown, clear-cut features. He was wearing a perfectly-tailored lightweight travelling suit in fawn, and he looked every inch the jetting young executive, off to finalise yet another million-dollar transaction.

His glance swept over Kate without expression. 'So you came?'

'Did you think I wouldn't?' She lifted her chin a fraction, remembering her resolution.

'No, I thought you would.' He walked towards the door and she moved quickly out of his path. 'Any girl would be stupid to turn down the offer of a free holiday in Hong Kong.'

She said coldly, 'My acceptance had nothing to do with a free holiday, you know that.'

'No? Oh well, have it your way. We'll have to see how it works. My sister will take things on from here, won't you, Polly? I'll expect you out in H.K. in due course.'

A bell sounded. 'That'll be my transport,' he said. 'I'll be on my way.'

'Just a minute,' said Kate.

Paul Caister looked at her as at a docile puppy who had just snapped at him, but he gave her his attention. 'Yes?'

'There's one rather important thing—what do I tell my brother?'

He raised dark brows. 'Tell him? Tell him to get on with the job, of course, and keep his hands out of the petty cash drawer in future.'

She wanted desperately to strike that hard, sneering face. She clenched her hands tightly and pressed on, 'But he can't just walk in as if nothing had happened. The head of his department knows about it and——'

He moved his broad shoulders impatiently. 'That's all been dealt with. Now, is there anything more?'

'No, nothing.' She hated him, his hard arrogance, his reducing of her to nothing.

'Good.' He looked towards his sister, across the room. 'Cheero, Polly, thanks for your help.' His glance just skimmed over Kate.

Polly came across the room, her dark eyes dancing. 'Aren't you going to kiss your fiancée goodbye, then?'

His eyes gleamed. 'You think of everything, don't you, sister mine? Nevertheless, it's quite an idea. We must start somewhere, mustn't we?'

Kate's mind went quite blank as he moved towards her and put a hand behind her shoulder, drawing her against him with a steady strength that was impossible to resist. He looked down into her face and she could feel her whole body recoil as his mouth drew nearer to hers. She pressed her lips tightly together, feeling a trembling start inside her, a fluttering weakness in her limbs.

His eyes moved to her mouth as he murmured, 'A little practice might be in order before we appear in public as a loving couple,' and brushed his lips against hers gently, sensuously, leisurely.

She gave a little gasp. If she had been in any state to think about it she would have expected his kiss to be as brief, as perfunctory as possible, to match everything else in his treatment of her up to now. Instead it was slow, deliberately arousing. She had never been kissed like that before and her senses swam. It was a tantalising kiss, a beginning without an end, and suddenly she wanted it to go on, to deepen and harden. Her eyes closed and she responded as naturally and inevitably as if he had been her lover and not a man she scarcely knew and heartily disliked.

When he let go her hand reached for the back of a chair and clung on to it. He stood looking down at her, his dark eyes narrowed and glittering beneath their thick lashes. 'Well, well, not a little grey mouse after all but a pink sugar mouse.' He flicked the collar of her rose-coloured sweater and his fingers lingered against her chin for a moment. 'I shall have to take care not to eat it up, shan't I?'

He turned his gaze upon Polly, who was watching this performance with interest. 'Do your best with our little mouse,' he said. 'Dress it up prettily and despatch it according to plan.'

He walked to the door, picked up his air-travel cases and lifted a hand in farewell. Kate had time to notice the mocking smile that touched the corners of his mouth before he went out. She stared dazedly at the door he had just closed, aware that Polly had spoken to her but that the words hadn't registered. 'I'm sorry?' she queried, feeling a fool.

Polly was smiling broadly. 'Knocked you off your balance, did he? Paul's an expert, I'm given to understand by his girl-friends. What I said was would you like some coffee?'

'Oh. Oh, yes that would be lovely, thank you.' Kate followed the beautifully-poised black-suited back down the long room, wishing for just half Polly's composure.

Polly poured coffee into a beaker and said, 'I'll have to go down and open up soon, but I don't suppose I'll have anyone in yet. Let's just sit and drink our coffee, then you can come down with me and see what you fancy in the way of clothes. Paul's given me a hefty cheque, so you can let yourself go.'

Kate sank into a chair. That kiss, coming so unexpectedly and on top of all the stress of the last few days, had left her feeling totally drained, but she was coming back to normal now. She blinked at Polly. 'Sorry to be so woozy, I'll wake up soon.' Her voice sounded far away.

Polly nodded vigorously. 'I know, it's all been a bit sudden. My brother isn't exactly noted for dawdling, once he makes up his mind about anything. You'd get the impression that he acted on impulse, but not on your life! That man's brain can calculate the odds like a human computer. He amazes me constantly.'

Kate firmed her pretty mouth. That kiss had been a calculated kiss, she recognised now, and she didn't like that sort of kiss at all, she decided. 'He's wrong about one thing, though. I'm not a pink sugar mouse, or a grey church mouse. In fact, I'm not any sort of mouse.'

Polly Chard looked at her thoughtfully. 'No, I can see that now.'

'I suppose he got that impression,' Kate continued, 'because when I saw him at his office yesterday I was nervous and at a disadvantage. You know the facts?'

'About your brother? Yes, Paul told me, and I think your brother ought to be grateful to you.'

'He'd better be,' Kate said darkly. 'He's quite old enough to be responsible for his own actions. But of course I didn't do it for Jerry's sake, it was for my father—he's been ill and I knew he couldn't take the strain of a court prosecution, he would have felt the disgrace terribly. Then when Jerry had worked himself into a high temperature I offered to come and see your brother instead and explain about my father. I don't think I was very hopeful really, and I was right. Your brother didn't want to listen, he was very—crushing.'

Polly pulled a wry face. 'I know, he can be.'

'So when he came up with this proposal that he would give Jerry another chance if I would go out to Hong Kong to act as his fiancée for a month I hadn't any choice but to agree. I suppose all this gave him the impression that I'm some sort of a meek little mouse.'

Polly chuckled. 'I can see that Paul's got quite a surprise coming to him!'

'Oh, I'll keep my side of the bargain and I won't be any trouble to him—unless he asks for it, that is. Could I ask you just one thing, though?'

'Ask away.' Polly put down her coffee beaker and prepared herself to listen, dark head tilted, small face lively with interest.

'Do you know why he needs a fiancée for a limited period? The usual ploy is to put up a Keep Off notice to predatory females, I imagine, but I should have thought your brother was perfectly capable of delivering the brush-off himself.'

There was a short silence, then Polly said, 'I don't know, I wish I did. Paul doesn't talk about his personal affairs—certainly not about his girls. And he's had plenty, of course. I mean—well, you've seen him.'

'Yes,' said Kate. She hadn't liked what she'd seen, but she had to admit the man's masculine charisma—that blend of masterful arrogance and sheer sexual magnetism that still has the power to make women grovel. But not me, she vowed. Not on your life, Mr Paul Caister.

Polly got up and carried the coffee beakers into the adjoining kitchen and Kate followed her.

'He's always been a workaholic,' his sister mused. 'I didn't think any girl would catch him. Then he came back from Hong Kong a couple of weeks ago and—wham!—within days he announced that he was going to get married. She was a model, a girl called Gabrielle. I introduced them myself. I didn't know her well, but she was—is— the most gorgeous thing imaginable, one of your willowy, raven-haired, white-skinned, violet-eyed beauties. Paul was quite besotted.' She chuckled. 'I never thought I'd see the day that Paul was crazy about a girl. He was planning to take her out to Hong Kong with him when he went back.'

She swilled the beakers and set them to drain. Kate waited.

'He took her out to dinner the night before last,' Polly went on. 'He'd bought her the most beautiful ring, he showed it to me. Well, around ten o'clock he was back here looking angrier than I've ever seen him look. He slammed the ring down and said, "It's off, Polly. Don't ask me why, and don't speak of it again, please." He looked as if he'd got a volcano inside him, waiting to burst into flames. He's not a man to take kindly to being turned down.'

She shrugged. 'That's the story, as far as I know it, except that he's been in a foul mood ever since. I expect you noticed.'

They went back into the living room and Kate asked, 'But why—why *me*?'

'Don't ask me why—Paul's a law unto himself, as they say. Probably because his buddies out in Hong Kong will be expecting him to produce his fiancée. He's in touch all the time by phone and telex—he's bound to have told them. He'd look silly if he had to tell them she'd turned him down—he wouldn't like that.'

'But nobody will believe I'm a glamorous model. To him I'm a mouse, you heard what he said. Grey mouse or pink mouse, take your choice.'

Polly looked hard at her. 'I'm not so sure. Moonlight fair hair, perfect skin, good bone structure, eyes like the poets say—you know, clear mountain pools. Oh yes, my girl, you've definitely got something. Hasn't anyone ever told you you're beautiful?'

'Well——' Kate grinned '—men say all sorts of nice things when they want something. You don't have to believe them.'

Polly spluttered with laughter. 'Bright as well—the girl's got everything! I can't wait to choose some really super clothes for you.'

'It's very good of you to take so much trouble,' said Kate rather shyly.

'No trouble, it's business,' Polly assured her, 'and I enjoy my work. Besides, I owe Paul a favour. When my marriage broke up a couple of years ago he was rather marvellous to me. He set me up here, as a matter of fact. The place is going like a bomb now and I've nearly paid him back, but I'm very grateful. There's only the two of us—our parents both died years ago—and without Paul I'd have been sunk.' Her mischievous small face was clouded for a moment and then she smiled again. 'Come along downstairs and we'll take a look along the rails and you can bring a selection up here and have a good browse through them.'

She stood with her back to the window, eyes narrowed as they rested on Kate, like an artist about to start work on a masterpiece.

'A new hair style,' she mused. 'The latest in make-up. The right clothes. You're going to cause a riot in Hong Kong when you get out there.' She chuckled. 'Grey mouse indeed! Master Paul is going to get more than he bargained for!'

Polly was a dear and she was being kind, but not for a moment could Kate believe that Paul Caister would be impressed by any gloss that Polly could manage to put on her. Mouse she was to him and mouse she would stay.

But as she followed Polly down the steep flight of stairs and into the show-room she was remembering the way her knees had felt weak when he kissed her, how a sudden disturbing need she had never felt before had shaken her all through her body.

Oh no, Paul Caister would always get exactly what he bargained for—no more, no less.

But what about me? Kate thought, gripped by uneasy foreboding. Am I going to get more than I bargained for?

All of a sudden the weeks ahead were full of new and unknown hazards.

CHAPTER THREE

'NEARLY in now,' announced the grey-haired, intelligent-looking woman who had occupied the seat next to Kate's in the plane for the past twenty hours, since they took off from Heathrow in the pouring rain—was it this morning, or yesterday morning, or even the day before? Kate hadn't managed to work out the time-shift yet.

But one thing was certain, the sun was shining in Hong Kong. As she looked down through the small window as the jet lowered itself gently over the harbour the scene below seemed to glitter with light and colour.

Boats were everywhere, dotted over the dark blue water like confetti: dozens of small ones, hustling about busily, their bow-waves carving white plumes against the blue; larger, more stately ones, ferry boats or pleasure boats, perhaps chugging along with dignity; squat ones that might be hydrofoils; huge ungainly ones that looked like cargo boats; even a naval vessel of some sort, its flags fluttering proudly in the breeze. And further away a huddle of crafts of all shapes and sizes, their sails and awnings forming a solid mass when seen from this height.

Mrs Locke leaned sideways across Kate's shoulder to look down. 'Quite impressive from up here, isn't it? Even the junks and sampans in the floating villages look picturesque. Get nearer to them, though, and they're not so romantic— shabby and poor and patched—though very clean. The Chinese here are obsessive about washing their clothes. They festoon them in every available place.'

Kate gazed down, fascinated, but with a sense of disbelief. At times, in the past ten days, it had seemed almost impossible that it would really happen; but now here she was, in a huge jet plane, hovering above Hong Kong—a new girl with the fabulous new clothes that Polly had chosen for her packed away in the luggage compartment; with an exciting new hair-style designed by Polly's hairdresser which gave Kate a start of surprise every time she caught sight of herself in a mirror; with a glittering great diamond ring on her engagement finger. ('Paul said to have it altered if it didn't fit. I'm afraid it's the one he chose for Gabrielle, but she never wore it—never even saw it, he said.') And with the sick feeling at the pit of her stomach growing worse and worse with every moment she got nearer to the time she would see Paul Caister waiting for her at the airport.

She gulped in a breath, still looking down. 'It's fascinating.'

Mrs Locke nodded approvingly. 'That's Hong Kong Island,' she said, and her rather dry and concise voice had a note of pleasure in homecoming. She waved down to where white skyscrapers clustered together against the background of a green, wooded hill. 'And that's the famous Victoria Peak. You don't get quite the right idea, seeing it from up here, it's extremely steep. See all those apartment blocks and villas dotted about among the trees? The Top People own the villas, the more humble, like myself, are lucky to rent an apartment there, but it's a splendid place to live.

The views are magnificent and one always feels—
alive, dynamic. Even an elderly lady like myself,'
she added with a wry smile.

Over the hours of the long flight Kate had
taken a liking for Mrs Locke. From the moment
they took their seats she had put Kate at her ease
and had established herself as a seasoned travel-
ler. 'It's very nice to have someone young and
pretty next to one,' she had observed, looking
with pleasure at Kate in the new cream linen
safari suit with the scarlet blouse.

They had exchanged the minimum of personal
details. Kate had said she was going out to Hong
Kong to join her fiancée, and very strange she had
felt when she said it. Mrs Locke's home was in
Hong Kong. She was a widow whose husband
had held a government post, and she had never
wanted to return to England for good, only now
and again to visit relatives.

'I'm a colonial,' she admitted. 'I cling to the
last of the British Empire and I love Hong Kong.
It has its own atmosphere—in some ways thriv-
ing and modern and forward-looking, in others—
well, the old colonial values and attitudes still live
on. The permissive society hasn't quite caught on
here.' She slanted a shrewd glance at Kate.
'Would you be a new woman?' she enquired with
a quirk of her expressive mouth.

Kate laughed, not in the least offended. 'I'm an
individual—I hope,' she said, and the older
woman nodded sagely and said, 'That's what I
thought.'

As soon as they were airborne Mrs Locke had
settled down with a book. 'You must excuse me if
I don't seem very sociable,' she announced pleasantly. 'And I sleep a lot on a plane.'

That had suited Kate, the last thing she wanted to do was to chat. She needed time to be quiet and try to adjust to the strangeness of her situation and what lay ahead. Right up to the time she got on the plane she had found herself hoping, at weak moments, that something catastrophic might happen that would make it quite impossible for her to go. But nothing had happened. In fact, everything had gone so smoothly that she had felt it was almost too bad to be true.

Aunt Ella had arrived and effortlessly taken over the running of the vicarage. Father had been touchingly delighted to see his sister again and seemed better and stronger. Jerry had returned to his job in a subdued frame of mind and appeared to be settling down at last. Mr Bruce, he told Kate, had been surprisingly decent about everything and had offered Jerry a training course on the practical side of the huge electronics business. Jerry had jumped at the opportunity of getting away from office routine and even in a few days had seemed more interested and involved in the work than Kate would have dared to hope.

There had had to be a certain amount of covering-up about the job that Kate was supposed to be going out to Hong Kong to do, but, although she felt a trifle uncomfortable about misleading Father and Aunt Ella, she had accepted the fact that it was unavoidable, and used her imagination freely in a good cause.

The hours she spent at Polly Chard's boutique in Mayfair, choosing clothes, had to be pure bliss to any girl, and she was buoyed up by Polly's flair and enthusiasm. 'With your shape you can carry off a softly classic silhouette,' Polly had announced. 'You don't need anything fussy. A crisp, clear look, that's what we'll aim at, to show off those gorgeous legs and play up to your eyes. Silk prints—nothing splashy—tailored linen—voiles. For evening we can let ourselves go with chiffon and ninon—mysterious, alluring!' She chuckled. 'Out with that mouse image for good! Jacques will do your hair marvellously and love it. It's got subtle silver-gilt lights in it – unusual – and one of the girls will find the right make-up and skin care for your very fine, clear skin. Oh, you're going to be a very lovely lady, Miss Kate Reynolds, when we've finished with you.'

Yes, thought Kate now, as she waited for the plane to land, Polly had been great fun, and a tower of strength too. She remembered their last conversation at the airport when they were waiting for her flight to be called. Father and Aunt Ella had wanted to come to Heathrow, but Kate had had to think up an excuse about a member of the corporation going with her. The fact was that Polly had had firm orders from Paul that she was to make absolutely sure that Kate was on the plane.

'He doesn't trust me not to renege?'

'After the way Gabrielle treated him I don't suppose he feels like trusting any woman,' said Polly. 'I still can't think why she turned him down—there was some talk about her and a Mexican oil millionaire, maybe that was it. Silly girl!'

Kate said nothing. Any mention of the exquisite model, Gabrielle, whom Paul had been crazy about and who had walked out on him, was inclined to make her curl up inside. Sitting beside Polly on the seat in the Departures Lounge she had a sudden terrible urge to call off the whole venture. Surely Paul Caister wouldn't take it out on Jerry now, at this late stage, and when he was out of the country and out of touch? But of course she couldn't. She had given her word and she had to go through with it, in spite of the horrid sinking feelings inside that kept assailing her.

Polly looked at her, eyebrows raised. 'You're nervous, aren't you, Kate? Don't be, there's no need.'

'How can I help it?' Kate wailed, 'I'm out of my depth. Your brother——'

'My brother is only a man,' smiled Polly. 'And you're a very lovely and very desirable young woman. Don't let yourself forget that.'

'He thinks I'm a mouse,' said Kate. 'He won't change his mind. He probably won't even look at me—he hasn't so far, only the merest glance. Oh, you've done wonders with me, Polly, and I'm terribly grateful. I feel a different person outside— all those lovely clothes and my hair and shoes and make-up and everything. I'll have more confidence to meet strangers and keep my end up. But your brother won't be fooled. I expect he'll still see me as I was that first time, all wet and bedraggled in that awful old grey mac—he won't notice the difference.'

'Then you must make him,' Polly said bluntly. 'Use shock tactics—*make* him sit up and notice you. Otherwise you're going to have a rotten time out there, if you let Paul bully you.'

Kate looked doubtful. 'I don't know if I'd have the nerve.'

'Of course you would.' Polly made it sound convincing. 'And anyway,' she added simply, 'what have you got to lose?'

'Ye-es.' Kate stared thoughtfully over the heads of the throng of moving bodies in the Departures Lounge. 'Yes,' she said again, and her eyes began to glitter. A slow smile broke over her face and she lifted her head so that the curves of pale hair moved sweetly against her neck. 'What have I got to lose?'

The two girls had looked at each other and begun to laugh.

Kate remembered that laughter now as the plane circled for the last time and lowered itself to touch down on the long concrete arm of runway that stretched out into the harbour. If she remembered to laugh, things couldn't be all that bad.

She and Mrs Locke pulled down their hand-luggage from the overhead locker. 'Shall we stay together until you meet your fiancé?' Mrs Locke suggested tentatively. 'Or would you rather make your own way?'

Kate accepted gratefully. 'Air travel is still pretty new to me. A weekend in Brittany last year is as far as I've been from home until now.'

She was glad of the older woman's expertise as they made their slow way from the plane, down the rubbery sleeve to the long crowded catwalk. Signs greeted them everywhere: Arrivals—Immigration Control—British Passports. 'They used to be quite fussy about Customs,' Mrs Locke raised her voice above the clatter, 'but there's no bother now unless you have something to declare; you just walk through.'

In a large hall they found trolleys, grabbed their luggage from the revolving carousel. And then, before Kate was quite ready for it, the dreaded moment was upon her as they passed along beside a rail, lined with eager faces that scanned each new arrival. Waves, beaming smiles, cries of excited welcome. Would he smile when he saw her? She hadn't seen him smile. She couldn't miss him, she thought a little faintly, he would be inches taller than anyone else along the rail.

'I don't think he's here,' she said at last.

They came to a standstill. 'He must be,' Mrs Locke said. 'You take a look around and I'll stay by your luggage.'

A voice came over the P.A. system. 'Will Miss Kate Reynolds, just arrived from London, please come to the Information Desk.'

'Ah!' said Mrs Locke, and led the way through the crowd.

At the desk Kate looked around and shook her head. Mrs Locke patted her arm, obviously thinking that she was desperately disappointed. 'I'll enquire for you, my dear, I'm sure there's no need to worry.'

She was back in a couple of minutes. 'I found him for you,' she said, and stood aside with a tactful smile.

Just behind her was a stocky young man with reddish hair and freckles. 'Miss Reynolds?' He was staring at Kate as if he couldn't believe what he saw. He cleared his throat and said hastily, 'I'm Josh Kinney, Mr Caister's P.A. Paul was very sorry he couldn't make it. He's held up at a conference and he asked me to come along and meet you.'

Mrs Locke looked from one to the other of them. '*Not* your fiancé? But you'll be all right now, so I'll be on my way. Nice to have met you, my dear. Come and look me up if you have a second of spare time. You'll find me in the phone book.'

And before Kate had time to thank her for her company and her help she mingled with the crowd, pushing her trolley determinedly before her.

The young man Josh was still looking somewhat stunned. 'Sorry about the mix-up,' he said. 'I was waiting at the rail—I thought I would recognise you from Paul's description, but I must have missed you. I hope you're not too disappointed.' He grinned at her, showing good, white even teeth.

'Of course not,' Kate said politely, smiling back. She wondered how Paul had described her. It seemed reassuring that she hadn't been recognisable from his description.

Josh picked up her two cases from the trolley. 'Shall we go, then? I've got Paul's car in the car park.'

He loaded the luggage into the trunk of a gloss white car and installed Kate in the passenger seat as if she were some beautiful and fragile object, which was a new experience for her. Little grey mice, she thought with a quirk of amusement, don't merit VIP treatment. But it was very pleasant, for once, and Josh Kinney was rather nice.

The temporary reprieve from confronting Paul had loosened her tension and she sat back in the soft comfort of the big car and looked out with interest as they drove along between blocks of apartments so high that they threw the road into deep shadow. She said, 'I love the way all the people here seem to hang out flagpole things from their windows to dry their washing on. It seems like a kind of welcome.'

Josh stole a quick glance at her as he manoeuvred the car into line. 'You merit a flag or two, Miss Reynolds,' he said, and then, as if afraid he had been too presumptuous, added in the same breath, 'We go through the tunnel here,' and the car slid down the smooth approach lane into the depths beneath the harbour.

They emerged on the opposite side into a wide dual carriageway, which surprised Kate as she had had an idea of Hong Kong as a maze of narrow streets brimming over with colourful humanity and exotic market-stalls and criss-crossed with gaudy banners hanging across the width of the street.

She said as much to Josh, who laughed and assured her that she would find as much Chinese 'atmosphere' as she wanted. 'But Hong Kong is twentieth century too. Wait until you see your hotel if you need convincing.'

When they drew up in the forecourt she admitted that he was right. The hotel was a soaring white giant, reaching up into the blue of the sky, gleaming with plate glass that twinkled and flashed in the sunshine. Josh helped her out of the car and she stood for a moment drinking in the sun and the clear freshness of the air. After the murky wet gloom of the London she had left behind it was all a trifle intoxicating.

Inside, the foyer seemed immense. A commissionaire—a tall, dignified Sikh in full regalia, magnificent in reds and golds and emerald greens with turban and sash—motioned them to one of the long reception counters.

'Oh, I do hope I'm really high up,' said Kate. 'What a view that must be!'

Her room turned out to be on the twenty-eighth floor, only two short of the top. Josh saw her installed with her luggage and said, 'I'll see you by the lift in the foyer when you're ready. Paul's joining us there when he's through with his meeting.'

Kate looked round the bedroom, which seemed to have everything necessary for comfort, with a good deal of luxury thrown in: a private bathroom, a writing table, TV, an armchair, a tiny fridge with an array of miniature bottles on top—soft drinks as well as the alcoholic kind. The bed was large and covered with an elaborately woven quilt, the fittings in dark polished wood that gave a feeling of Victorian splendour to the essentially modern room.

Kate looked down from the window on to a major road, but on her right she could glimpse the blue waters of the harbour and on her left she could just see the wooded green rise of the Peak.

She sighed. What a wonderful holiday she could have here—if it were really a holiday and if the daunting prospect of facing Paul Caister again weren't haunting her. 'Use shock tactics,' Polly had said. '*Make* him sit up and notice you.'

Suddenly the vitality of Hong Kong reached out and grabbed her. 'I will, Polly,' she said aloud. 'I really will. After all, as you said, what have I got to lose?'

She began to laugh as she peeled off her travelling clothes and went into the shower room.

Josh was waiting for her, standing under an enormous potted palm, when she came out of the lift twenty minutes later.

'Hullo again.' His nice brown eyes admired her. She was wearing one of Polly's favourite dresses—a pale green cotton, crisp as a lettuce leaf, with a daring neckline and wide revers. Its shape showed off her pretty curves to advantage.

'Paul not turned up yet?' She tried to sound as if she couldn't wait.

'Not yet, you'll have to put up with me for a bit longer,' he said cheerfully. 'Shall we have a drink?'

He led the way past a rickshaw, painted orange and hung with paper lanterns, into a bar at the centre of the vast lobby and ordered lemon and lime for both of them.

Kate sat back in a tubby basket chair and said, 'It's a very long meeting, surely? When did they start?' She had to keep up the fiction of impatience.

'Meetings out here are apt to get a bit drawn-out, and Paul had a few somewhat radical suggestions to make. Probably they're trying to argue him out of them. What a hope!' He grinned and took a long swig of his drink.

'What does he do, exactly? I don't know a thing about business,' Kate prevaricated with an apologetic smile.

'The full title is management consultant—and that means to the whole of the Corporation, not just out here.' She couldn't miss the note of respect in his voice.

'And you are one too? A management consultant?'

'Me? Good lord, no, I'm not nearly tough enough for that job. I'd be trodden underfoot in no time flat. I'm just Paul's dogsbody while he's working out here.'

'And the Barn Trekker Corporation—they're starting a branch to manufacture some special electronic gear in Hong Kong, is that it?'

He was looking rather curiously at her. 'That's right. But hasn't Paul told you about it?'

She shook her head. 'Not much. We talked mostly about ourselves.'

For no particular reason she felt the blood mounting into her cheeks. Well, that would give a good impression. A girl newly engaged and wildly in love ought to be allowed to blush.

'We haven't known each other very long,' she added, swirling her drink round in the tall glass and making the ice crackle.

Josh nodded. 'Yes, I guessed that. We all did. It quite knocked us back when we heard he was going to be married. I mean——' he added rather awkwardly—'we didn't expect—there wasn't any hint when he went home on leave a few weeks ago.'

'You didn't consider Paul the marrying type of man?' Kate asked demurely.

'Well, frankly—no.' He tossed down the remainder of his drink and added gallantly, 'But now that we've met, Miss Reynolds, I can see just why it happened.'

'Thank you, Josh, that's very sweet of you.' Her large grey eyes sparkled up at him like diamonds. 'And don't you think it would be more friendly to call me Kate?'

He leaned a little towards her to make his lowered voice audible about the chatter around. 'I think Paul's a lucky devil—Kate,' he said. 'And I also think he'll have to keep his eye on his girl while she's out here.'

He lifted his head, startled, as a deep voice from behind them said, 'Josh! What the hell are you playing at? I thought I asked you to meet

the plane, and here you are, fooling around
with——'

He stopped, walked round to the front of them,
staring down. For just a moment the sound of his
deep voice threatened to shatter Kate's resolve.
She swallowed, braced herself, and jumped to her
feet.

'Paul darling—how lovely!' she cried, and saw
his look of disbelief change to astonishment.

She took two steps into his arms and felt them
close round her, felt his mouth come down to
hers after a moment's hesitation. But this time his
kiss wasn't sensual and arousing, it was hard and
angry. She knew he was saying with his lips and
his arms, that were crushing her painfully, what
he couldn't say in words in Josh's company: Let
me call the tune.

But, angry or not, his kiss was doing very
strange things to her emotions and sending small
quivers up and down her spine. She wound her
arms round his neck and nestled against him, her
cheeks flushed and her satin hair, silver-gilt and
fragrant, brushing his cheek.

His hold tightened and she almost felt her
bones crack. 'Hey! I'm breakable,' she laughed
up at him, and saw, with a small feeling of
triumph, that she really had surprised him. He
was staring down at her with an unreadable
expression in his dark, liquid eyes. He's probably
furious inside, she thought exultantly. I've made a
good start.

She disengaged herself with a sigh and saw that
Josh was on his feet, examining the passing scene
in the foyer with apparent interest.

She turned back to Paul, laying a hand on his
arm. 'Darling, Josh looked after me beautifully,

when you couldn't come and meet me.'

'Good,' said Paul briefly. 'I think we can dispense with his help now.' The young man turned his attention back immediately. 'I've left a wad of stuff on my desk, Josh. See if you can get it into some sort of order before tomorrow morning, will you? I won't be coming back to the office again today.'

Josh nodded eagerly. 'No, of course not. I'll do that.' He shifted his weight from one foot to the other. 'Well, I'll be getting along, then. I'll be seeing you, Miss Reynolds.'

She smiled at him. 'The name is Kate. And thank you again, Josh. You've been very kind.'

He blinked twice, made a clumsy sort of bow and hurried away.

Paul was looking very dark. 'A splendidly convincing reunion scene! I see I shan't have to coach you. But there really isn't any need to turn on the charm for the benefit of my personal assistant.

She raised neat eyebrows and slid back into her chair. 'I think I should like another drink, please, Paul dear. Lime and lemon.'

He stood regarding her, his dark brows lowered. Then, without a word, he swung round and walked across to the bar. Kate watched him go, seeing the arrogance in the way he walked, the way he held his shoulders, the set of his dark head. A dangerous man to tangle with, she thought, and wondered if she had the nerve to keep it up.

He brought her drink and put it on the table before her. His own drink was in a tall glass too, but she guessed it was something more potent than lime and lemon. He sank into a chair oppos-

ite and drank in silence. Then he sat back, closing
his eyes. She saw the lines of fatigue on his face;
she had seen Father look like that—the tension of
hours of stress—only Father's stress had come
from worrying about other people, not from the
pressures of big business and making money.
Still, he really *did* look tired, and she couldn't
fight against a small welling-up of sympathy,
even if she did dislike the man and all he stood
for.

She sipped her drink and kept quiet until he
opened his eyes again. 'Was it difficult?' she enquired.

'Was what difficult?' She heard the impatience
in his voice and guessed that he was regretting
that he had landed himself with this unknown
female, however good his reason might have
been.

'The meeting,' she said calmly. 'Josh said
you'd been at it for hours and hours.'

He took out a clean handkerchief and passed it
over his face. 'Slightly stressful at times,' he said.
'I could do with a shower and a change.'

He gave her a doubtful glance. 'We'll go back
to my apartment now and then I can brief you
about the things you'll be expected to know.
We're invited out to dinner tonight.' He added as
an afterthought, 'Or do you want to sleep? Did
the flight put you out of gear?'

She smiled sweetly at him. 'No, thank you,
darling, I'm not a bit tired. I slept quite a lot on
the plane. And I don't think I'll get jet lag. I'm
not sure, of course, but I feel quite okay now. It
was so thoughtful of you to enquire,' she added
with a softly loving glance.

He clicked his tongue irritably. 'There's no

need to overdo the devotion, you know—certainly not when we're on our own.'

She put down her glass carefully. 'I'm supposed to be playing the part of an engaged girl, and I have to try to convince myself that I'm in love with you,' she said in a practical tone. 'As I don't find that very easy I shall need all the practice I can get, in private as well as in public.'

He gave her an odd glance. 'Do you find me so unlovable, then?'

She stood up, shaking out the crisp green skirt of her dress. 'I'm doing my best to see you as a wonderful person,' she said. 'So that's not a question I can answer yet.' She regarded him thoughtfully. 'You're very attractive,' she said, 'but I'm not at all sure about lovable.'

He moved his shoulders impatiently. 'This is a ridiculous conversation.'

'I agree,' she said. 'Shall we go, then?' She moved towards the entrance of the hotel, and out to where Josh had parked Paul's white car. He followed her in silence.

He drove quickly along the smooth wide freeways, his face grim. Kate looked about her with interest, not attempting to talk, and when the road began to rise steeply, twisting and turning, she knew they must be climbing the famous Peak that Mrs Locke had pointed out to her. The apartment building, when they finally turned off the road into the short driveway, must have been high up on the hill, for the sweep of view below— the blue harbour crowded with shipping, the high white buildings, standing up stiff and straight like upended pencil boxes—was quite breathtaking.

Kate got out of the car and stood looking down

through the trees, drinking it in. 'Aren't you lucky to live here?' she said softly. 'What a fabulous place!'

Paul slammed the car door and locked it. 'Let's cut the social chit-chat, shall we?' he said wearily, and led the way into the building.

She shrugged. Her enthusiasm hadn't been social chit-chat, it had been spontaneous and genuine, but if he preferred silence, then that was all right with her.

A lift shot them upwards to somewhere that must have been near the top of the building, and Paul put his key into the door to the left of the small landing. The apartment was furnished in comfortable, completely European fashion, not a touch of Chinese about it. Kate thought that was rather a pity, when there must be so many fascinatingly different objects one could buy here, but she kept that opinion to herself and sat down at one end of the sofa he indicated, looking out to a balcony, and with that wonderful view spread far below.

'Drink?' he asked, going to a built-in cupboard across the room.

'No, thanks,' she said. 'What I'd like more than anything else would be a cup of tea. Would that be possible?'

'Tea!' He straightened and closed the cupboard door. 'A brilliant idea, why didn't I think of it? Madam's wish is my command.' He went into an adjoining room which Kate saw, through the open door, was a fitted kitchen.

'Can I help?' she called to him.

'Not this time. Another time you may add the domestic touches, perhaps.' She heard the tap hiss as he filled the kettle, the clink of cups and saucers. She wished he wouldn't find it necessary to sound either angry or ironic every time he spoke to her.

Presently he carried a tray in and put it down on the sofa table in front of her. Then he sank into the cushioned depths of the sofa, leaving a wide gap between them, and stretched out his long legs. 'I'll allow you to do the pouring out,' he said lazily.

Kate wasn't sure whether that was intended to be said as a kind of joke or not. She wasn't sure of anything where this man was concerned. She poured two cups and pushed one along the table to him. They both drank in silence.

Paul put his cup down. 'That was good, I shouldn't have thought of tea myself. It's useful to have a little woman about the place.'

She looked at him over the rim of her cup. 'Need you?' she said.

'Need I what?'

'Need you adopt this silly, patronising tone every time you speak to me? You've made it clear that you think of me as a little grey mouse, a non-entity, but if you go on treating me like one aren't your friends and colleagues out here going to think it a bit odd? I mean, nobody would believe that Paul Caister would choose to marry a mouse, surely?'

He turned dark, brooding eyes on her. 'You've been thinking it all out very cleverly, have you? Was that why you put on the big act at the hotel? Practising the glamour and allure on young Josh Kinney? Not too difficult to dazzle Josh, hardly worth the effort, I'd have thought.' He took out a silver case and selected a thin cheroot from it. 'May I?'

She watched him flick a lighter, his slim brown fingers moving with economical strength, and wondered if she were simply being idiotic to challenge a man like this in any way—a man so superbly confident, arrogant, self-sufficient. For a moment her resolution wavered. But only for a moment. Then she said quietly, 'I wasn't putting on an act with Josh—only with you.'

Their eyes met in a long, taut silence. She felt her inside begin to quiver, but she thought desperately, If I give in now at the beginning I've lost. I might as well *be* a mouse.

Somehow she managed to hold his look, even to curve her lips with a very small smile.

It was Paul who broke the silence. 'So be it, you've got your message over. You have to make a terrific effort to convince yourself that you might be in love with me, is that it?'

'Yes,' she said.

'I see.' He nodded thoughtfully and there was an odd gleam in his eyes. 'It's an obstacle, but not insurmountable. Perhaps I could help you to change your mind?' Deliberately he put down his cigar and moved along the sofa towards her.

She went rigid. She knew he was going to kiss her—she knew that she had invited it—worst of all, she knew she wanted it.

Slowly and carefully he took the empty cup out of her hand and put it back on the table. Then he turned to her, one hand on either side of her resting on the back of the sofa. Involuntarily she shrank into a corner as he leaned over her.

'No!' she gasped faintly.

'Oh yes.' His voice was deep and very soft, almost threatening. 'It was your own idea that you needed some practice in being my fiancée—

with all that that involves,' he reminded her.

One hand went under her chin, lifting her face for his mouth to meet hers, to touch, to explore. It was like that first kiss he had given her, tantalising, arousing, and it went through her like a series of electric shocks. She wanted to resist, but her pulses were beating furiously and she felt her lips soften and part beneath his.

She lay back helplessly against the sofa while his hands stroked her neck, moved across her bare shoulder to find the sensitive spot beneath her hair at the back. She shivered violently and tried to pull away, but his body was pressed against hers and his other arm held her firmly at the waist.

He was very deliberate, very leisurely about it, savouring the kiss as if it were some rare delicacy, and when at last he took his mouth away he smiled and said, 'How was that? Did it break the ice at all?'

Break the ice? There was a gaping crack right down the middle of it, Kate admitted to herself wildly. But she wasn't going to admit it to him; if he thought he could dominate her by his sheer *machismo* he was wrong.

'Not that I noticed,' she said, relieved that her voice sounded cool and indifferent. 'Anyway, I wouldn't fall in love with a man merely because I found him physically attractive.'

'Really?' His smile was frankly mocking now. 'That's most interesting. What test would you apply, then?'

'I haven't considered it—the matter hasn't arisen,' she said distantly. The words sounded stilted and ridiculous. She added quickly, 'I've always thought I'd just—know.'

'Ah! The famous feminine intuition! Well, you'll give me due warning if it looks likely to happen while you're still engaged to me, won't you? I should have to consider the matter.'

Just for a moment she saw a hard bleakness pass over his face, and she thought of Gabrielle, the girl who had walked out on him. Had he really cared all that much? Was he capable of being crazily in love with a woman? And how would he show it? The pictures that ran into her mind sent the blood coursing hotly through her body.

She pulled herself up very straight and said, 'I promise to give you notice.'

There was a short silence. That part of the proceedings seemed to be over. Paul pushed his cup along the table and said, 'Pour me some more tea, will you, and then I'll take my shower.'

He drank it walking towards the door. 'I won't be long,' he said. 'There are some magazines on the desk over there.'

But Kate didn't want to look at magazines. Alone, she sat staring down through the window at the view below, the twisting white road winding up the hill, in and out between the trees; the dark blue water of the busy harbour; the hazy coastline of the mainland beyond; seeing it in a bemused way through the confusion of her thoughts.

She had known from the first moment she agreed to play this game that it would be difficult. Playing any sort of game with Paul Caister would present difficulties, because he wasn't a loser. But now she saw that there would be more than difficulties, there would be dangers, and that the dangers would come from herself, just as much as from him.

To fall in love with this man would be to ask for a black misery that she could only guess at, because he wasn't going to fall in love with her. This was a game that demanded coolness and nerve and self-control on her part. She could only hope she had what it would take.

He came out of the bathroom. He had changed into black trousers, fitting immaculately at his slim waist and hips, and a white silk shirt open at the neck. His hair gleamed wetly. He looked, Kate had to admit, devastatingly handsome.

'Phew! That's better.' He sank into a chair beside the sofa. 'Stewing over reports in a committee room all day isn't my idea of fun. I prefer to be active. Now then, let's get down to details. I'd better explain to you about——'

'Just a minute.' She lifted a hand. 'Before you start issuing your instructions, there's something I'd like to say.'

He looked surprised. 'Yes? What is it?'

'I'd like to let my people at home know, as soon as possible, that I've arrived safely. As I told you, my father hasn't been well and my aunt, who has come to look after things while I'm away, is elderly too. I'm sure they would be relieved to know that I'm safe and sound. In our sort of life we don't fly across the world every day, you know,' she added without sarcasm, purely as a statement of fact.

'Of course you must get in touch,' he said quickly and with such reasonableness that she wondered if she were dreaming. 'I'm sorry, I should have thought of it before.'

She glanced at him, amazed, but he was perfectly serious. She said, 'Thank you. Which would be the best way—would an air-mail letter take long? Or a cable or something?'

'You have a phone at home? Yes? Well then, speak to them, you can't get anything more immediate than that.'

'Oh, could I?' Her eyes lit up eagerly. 'But—but wouldn't it be terribly expensive?'

He smiled faintly. 'I take it you're not going to have a long heart-to-heart talk with anyone. What's the number?'

She told him and he scribbled it down on a pad by the telephone. He said, 'We're seven hours on here—it'll be about eleven o'clock in the morning in England. Will there be someone at home?'

'Oh yes, I'm almost sure there will.' She watched him as he turned to the instrument and began to dial. He leaned back lazily, crossing his long legs, the picture of a man with everything under control—even the telephone wouldn't dare to serve him with a wrong number, she thought wryly.

He waited, very still, and from across the room she could hear the clicks as the call went through all its connections. In an amazingly short time he said, 'Yes, just a moment, please, Miss Reynolds would like to speak to you.' He got up from the chair, holding out the receiver. 'Your aunt, I think.'

She took the receiver and sank into the chair. 'Aunt Ella? Yes—this is Kate. Isn't it extraordinary? Yes, of course I'm in Hong Kong. Look, this is costing an awful lot. It's just to say I've arrived and everything's O.K. and I'll write. How's Father? Good—and you? Right, I'll ring off now. Goodbye, Aunt dear, look after yourself.'

She replaced the receiver and stared at Paul. 'That was amazing! I don't think my poor aunt believed it was really me, in Hong Kong.'

'Direct dialling—the wonders of modern technology!' he drawled. He was looking hard at her. 'Your eyes glitter like diamonds when you're excited,' he said.

He was watching her under lowered lids and she was so taken aback that she had no response ready and to her horror she felt her cheeks begin to burn. His kiss had been one thing, but this was quite different. He almost looked as if he really meant it, as if he intended to pay her a genuine compliment.

She walked a little dazedly back to the sofa. 'Thank you,' she said uncertainly.

He sat down again opposite and the dark eyes were fixed upon her flushed cheeks, and dancing wickedly. 'If *you* need practice to convince yourself that I'm lovable, then why shouldn't I be allowed the same, if you follow me.'

It was like a douse of cold water. How stupid could you get? she asked herself angrily. She certainly wouldn't make *that* mistake again.

'No reason at all,' she said coolly. 'It surprised me, that's all. A compliment—coming from *you*!'

His eyes narrowed mockingly. 'Oh, I do pay compliments to ladies now and again, you know.'

'Yes—but not to little grey mice. Or pink sugar mice either,' she added.

He picked up his cigar and coaxed it back into glowing life. 'Why not? I rather like mice of any hue. And anyway, Polly has managed to wipe out the mouse image very successfully. The mouse has become a kitten, developed claws, and gone on the attack.'

She stared at him coldly. 'A whimsical idea, but rather a blow to the theory of evolution, surely?'

He raised dark eyebrows. 'An educated kitten, it seems!'

Kate lost her temper. She almost forgot it wasn't Jerry sitting there, teasing her. 'Oh, shut up!' she flashed at him in sisterly rage.

He burst out laughing. 'That's cleared the air. Now, let's get on with the briefing, shall we?'

Kate folded her hands on her lap. 'Certainly,' she said in the voice of a trained secretary.

This, she reminded herself, was what she had come for—to do a job. An unusual job, certainly, and not without its difficulties and dangers. And one of the first rules for a good employee was not to allow yourself to become emotionally involved with your employer.

Already, she thought dismally, she had broken half the rules in the book. She had started by hating and resenting him; gone on to admit—grudgingly—his masculine charisma; reacted to his kisses with a shattering inner turmoil; allowed him to needle her until she lost her temper.

She would do better, she decided, when they were with other people. There was something altogether too intimate about being here with him, in his private apartment.

She was very thankful that they would be dining with others and not having a party for two.

CHAPTER FOUR

PAUL leaned back in his chair and drew pleasurably on his cigar. 'The party's being given by the Nichols—Michael and Laura. Michael Nichols is the head of our Hong Kong Branch, and one of the best. I value his friendship highly. Laura is—well——' for a moment the dark eyes were veiled '—not altogether easy. But you'll see for yourself. She's very spectacular. There'll be one or two other guests, I expect. I don't know who they've invited.'

'And I'm to be on show, as your new fiancée?' Kate queried.

He nodded. 'I gather that it's to welcome you and——' he grinned with faint derision '—to take a look at the girl I'm going to marry. There's still a touch of the old-style colonial society out here. Everyone is vitally concerned with everyone else's business.'

She remembered that Mrs Locke had warned her about that. It didn't help her confidence one little bit. 'Well, what's my brief? How, exactly, do you suggest that I behave?' She laid one arm along the back of the sofa, crossed her legs, and sat back. She hoped she looked nonchalant and slightly amused by the whole thing. She certainly didn't feel it.

Paul's dark eyes passed over her and he frowned. 'When I thought you were a mouse I was going to suggest that you merely smiled prettily and spoke when you were spoken to. But

I can see that's not going to fill the bill with Kate Mark Two.'

Her mouth twitched. 'It doesn't sound like my idea of an exciting evening.'

He looked keenly at her. 'Is that what you're looking for—excitement?'

'You promised me a holiday,' she said. 'Surely a holiday contains some excitement. It would be terribly dull otherwise.'

There was a short silence, then he said, 'Fair enough. But let it be understood that—if you mean what I think you mean by excitement—it'll be provided by me.' Suddenly the dark eyes smouldered. 'No fooling around, Kate. If you let me down, by God, I'll——'

She saw that his fingers were clenched tightly on the thin cigar as he stubbed it out. 'I won't let you down,' she said quietly, and went on without giving him time to pursue the subject, 'I told Josh that we'd only met each other quite recently. I thought it would make things easier if we weren't supposed to know a great deal about each other yet.'

He nodded. 'That figures. I've a hazy idea about how your family is constituted. You've met Polly, who's all the family I've got. That's about it.'

She asked, 'Do you stay with Polly when you're in England, or have you a place of your own?'

'I've a cottage in the country, for the times when I'm able to relax. I did have a flat in town, but the lease fell due just before I came out here a few months ago. Since then I've been using Polly's flat for the short times I've been home. When I finish here finally I'll probably find another place in London—if I'm going to be there long enough, that is. I never know.'

She said, 'Where's your cottage?'

'Devon. Not far from Torquay, a little place called Ashburton.'

'Ashburton!' She clapped her hands, her eyes shining, her pose of nonchalance forgotten. 'Oh, it's a lovely place, I know it well. We used to live quite near there before my father took this living in London. I was brought up there and went to school in Torquay. What a coincidence! We could——'

'We could—what?' His dark look held mockery.

Her eyes were wide, her cheeks pink with confusion. 'How stupid of me! I got carried away by the thought of Devon.'

'You should get carried away more often,' he said blandly. 'It suits you.'

There was a calculating look in his eyes that made her heart begin to thump uncomfortably. She rushed into small talk. 'We used to go to Ashburton to picnic by the river. And once we went from school to see the Iron Age hill fort. We used to love to ride on the Dart Valley Railway. The steam trains were such fun.' Her voice sounded two tones higher than usual.

His long, stern mouth was touched by a smile. 'If you're a good girl and do a good job here for me, I'll take you for a holiday there when we get back to England.'

She stared at him, not pretending to misunderstand. 'I didn't mean that,' she said distantly. 'And you know I didn't.'

His dark eyes moved over her thoughtfully, taking in everything: the new sleek, fashionable hair-do that Polly's hairdresser had created for her, the pretty figure moulded softly beneath the crisp green dress, the long silken line of her legs where her skirt fell away at her knees, down to the elegant high-heeled white sandals with their single narrow strap.

'It might be quite—exciting,' he drawled.

What she saw in his eyes made her shiver inside with a weakness she couldn't control. But at least she could control her words.

'Look, let's get one thing clear,' she said quickly, 'I'm not in the market for an affair while I'm here. I'm ready to play at being in love and that's the limit. Anyway,' she reminded him, 'I'm not your type, you told me so yourself.'

He sighed. 'We say the most stupid things sometimes. Okay, have it your way, we'll just play at being in love, as you say. I foresee that even that might be quite rewarding.'

He stood up. 'Now, I suppose I'd better get you back to your hotel. You'll want to change for the evening. I'm quite looking forward to seeing what glamour Polly has provided—the little number you're wearing now is quite an aperitif.' His eyes moved down to linger on the neckline of the bodice and the revers that hinted at, rather than disclosed, the soft swelling curve of her breasts.

Kate stood up too, turning away from him. Her knees suddenly felt like indiarubber and she swayed unsteadily, giving a little gasp of surprise. He was beside her immediately, one arm holding her strongly, which had the effect of making her feel more dizzy than ever.

'Are you all right?' He looked concerned and his face was very close to hers.

She shook her head as if she could shake off a threat. 'Yes—quite all right now, it was just a spot of jet-lag, I expect,' she improvised. 'I hadn't felt it until this moment.'

Was she going to go on being forced to tell lies to this man? Finding excuses for her disastrously overwhelming response to his physical presence? It was a frightening prospect.

He was still holding her round the waist, still looking faintly anxious. He was so close that she could see the separate hairs of his eyebrows, the way they rose thickly and then fell again, making little tents over the dark, brooding eyes. 'Are you quite sure you're up to this party tonight?' he asked. 'We could easily get out of going if you like.'

'No—really. It was only a passing thing. I'm absolutely fine now.'

His eyes searched her face doubtfully. She wished he hadn't got this way of being kind when she didn't expect it. It seemed out of character and it played havoc with her resolve to go on dis-liking the man.

'Well—if you're sure. I'll go and put on a jacket and tie and we'll be on our way, then.'

He went out of the room and came back a minute or two later wearing a white evening jacket over his black trousers, and knotting an orange silk tie—a rich, vibrant colour against the stark white of his shirt. He looked every inch the successful top executive, Kate told herself, trying to feel a kind of contempt for what must surely be his values. Values that must be so very different from the ones with which she had been brought up. Values that she must hang on to, at any cost, while she was here. She had seen enough of Paul

Caister to know that letting herself fall in love with him would be asking for what, in days gone by, would have been called a broken heart. Hearts weren't supposed to break in these more realistic times, but Kate had a feeling that the anguish hadn't changed all that much.

He glanced round the apartment. 'Shall we be on our way, then? I'm afraid you're going to have to do quite a bit of shuttling back and forth between here and your hotel, but the taxi service is quite good when I'm not available. If it had been London I could have put you up here. I've got a spare room.'

He opened the door for her to pass through, and paused to lock it. 'But that wouldn't do at all here. It would lead to complications.'

'Gossip?'

'Oh yes, that. But something more hard to handle.' He pressed the lift button and stood staring musingly at it.

'I do wish you wouldn't talk in riddles,' Kate said crossly, and felt her heart lurch as she realised, too late, the implications of his words.

'It isn't a riddle. What usually happens when a man and an attractive girl share an apartment?'

She groped for—and somehow found—her composure again. 'It only happens if they're both willing,' she said coolly.

'And you wouldn't be?'

'Certainly not!'

'A pity! We might have made your stay quite memorable. Contrary to what I expected when I started this thing, I now find that I seem to have a very disturbing young woman on my hands.'

Kate felt a sudden unnerving spurt of something that felt like joy, but that was absurd, of course. The way Paul was looking down at her, his dark eyes full of mockery, told her that this conversation was not to be taken seriously.

'And does that put you out?' she said calmly. 'Would you like to send me home again?'

'Would you like to go?'

She pretended to consider it, but inside she was screaming, No, no, no! 'If I said Yes, would you send me back?' she asked.

His eyes met hers and then slowly lowered themselves to fix on her mouth. 'No,' he said.

The lift arrived and they got in. Kate moved as far away as possible—which wasn't very far in the small space—and added, 'I suppose if I suddenly disappeared again that would defeat the object of the exercise. People would want to know why.'

'Exactly,' he said in an offhand tone, passing from the personal to the impersonal in a flash. She was beginning to recognise this habit of his now. 'There would be Talk; in other words Tittle-Tattle——' he grimaced fastidiously '—something I detest. That's one reason why I brought you out here.'

'Is it?' she said coolly. 'I wondered when I was going to be told the reason.'

'Didn't Polly tell you?'

They emerged from the lift and walked out into the evening dusk. After the air-conditioned apartment the atmosphere felt warm and humid. 'Polly said she didn't really know.' Kate glanced up at the dark, hard profile of the man walking beside her and added, 'She told me that you'd been engaged recently but it had been broken off. She guessed that you might want to have a stand-in fiancée, to save you having to waste time answering a lot of questions.'

His expression told her nothing. 'That's about fifty per cent of it,' he said.

'And the other fifty per cent? Am I to know that too?'

He opened the door of the car for her to get in. 'We'll talk about that some other time,' he said.

An hour or so later Kate stepped out of the lift and stood alone in the vast hotel lobby. People seethed round her—drifting about, standing in groups, hurrying purposefully towards the lifts or the long reception desks, laughing, talking. The tempo of the day was changing. Those who had been engaged all through the hot, humid hours in business, or in determined sightseeing, were relaxing with relief into the more leisurely evening time.

Paul had told her that he must return to his office for a while and had arranged to meet her in the lobby at half-past seven, giving her time for a rest before she need begin to dress for the evening. Her eyes searched the moving crowd for him now but didn't find him. The sudden disappointment that she felt surprised her. Only a few hours ago she had been dreading seeing him again, but now she found herself looking eagerly for him. It was ridiculous.

She turned her gaze on the people around her. Many of the women were already dressed for the evening in elegant affairs of silks or chiffons. This was a modern, Western-style hotel, but there were plenty of Chinese around, the men neat and carefully dressed and attentive, the women wearing their exquisite cheongsams, embroidered in glowing reds and yellows and blues, their black hair shining like ravens' wings, the little stiff stand-up collars giving an exotic touch to their smooth golden necks and arms.

Minutes passed, but Paul didn't come. Kate paced backwards and forwards before the lifts, aware of the glances she was attracting from some of the men who passed her, not yet quite at ease in the new self-image that she and Polly between them had created. Before she left her bedroom her mirror had assured her that she looked good—equal to playing the part of Paul Caister's fiancée. She was wearing her favourite of the dresses she had brought with her, cream jersey crêpe with a deep cowl neck draped low over her prettily-rounded breasts, and a wide, softly-pleated belt that hugged her slim waist and fastened with a gold, ornate clip in front. She carried a floating georgette scarf in the hand that held her gold kid evening bag, and on her feet were the most beautiful sandals she had ever seen—dull gold, with interlaced narrow straps and delicately high heels. She had arranged her fine, pale-gold hair in its new style—a soft swathe across her head from each side, forming a kind of pleat over one eyebrow and taken back from her pretty ears. She hadn't yet got used to the air of sophistication it gave her, but at least it all added up to the picture of the kind of girl Paul Caister might conceivably choose to marry.

Where *was* he? She wished he would come. She felt conspicuous, standing alone here, growing more and more conscious of the looks she was attracting.

Suddenly, and quite without warning, she had a feeling of near-panic, as though a cold cloud had enveloped her. She knew it was irrational, but she couldn't help it. In the pleasantly air-conditioned atmosphere she felt icy cold and dithery and she had a horrible feeling she was going to faint and make a fool of herself.

She leaned against the wall beside the lift, fighting off the sensation of lightheadedness, telling herself not to be an idiot, her eyes looking for Paul with a desperate eagerness.

Then she saw him coming towards her, walking swiftly and purposefully, and the relief was overwhelming. Hardly knowing what she was doing, she almost ran to him, holding out her hands. The blood had come back to her head quickly, giving her a slightly tipsy feeling.

'Paul—oh, Paul!' she murmured, her face radiant, her wide-set grey eyes brilliant.

He took her hands and stood looking into her face in a puzzled kind of way, the dark crooked eyebrows lifted. Then, very slowly, he drew her hands against his jacket and bent his head to kiss her.

She pulled away a little, her lips tingling from his kiss, her heart thudding unevenly. 'I—I was beginning to get jittery,' she began to explain in a high, quick voice. He was looking so surprised at the enthusiasm of her greeting that she felt some explanation was necessary. 'I thought perhaps I'd mistaken the time or something.' She took a couple of steps back and the skirt of her dress clung sensuously at waist and hips. 'Will I do?'

'You look very beautiful.' His voice was deep and his eyes had their brooding look behind their thick dark lashes. He lifted a hand and touched her cheek. 'I didn't realise how perfect your skin is.'

She was suddenly bereft of breath and she felt idiotically that it would be the most natural thing in the world if she caught his hand and held it against her mouth. Steady on, she warned herself. This is all part of a game, remember?

Somehow she produced a mischievous little grin. 'Well done,' she murmured. 'You're getting into the part beautifully. But enough is enough.' She glanced round the lobby to see if his friends appeared to be waiting for him. 'Where are we going?'

He hadn't taken his eyes from her face and he wasn't returning her smile. 'I know where I'd like to take you,' he said, with meaning.

She felt her cheeks flame. 'I said enough is enough,' she exclaimed in playful rebuke. 'And I want my dinner, I'm hungry.'

Paul drew in a breath and his mood seemed to change. 'Okay, okay, I get the message. Mike Nichols is waiting out in the car for us. The others are meeting up with us at the restaurant.' He took her hand, twining his fingers with hers, and led her towards the door.

Kate liked Michael Nichols from the first moment she saw him, leaning against Paul's big white car, the light pouring out from the hotel frontage showing him as a tall, rather gaunt figure with thin brown hair and twinkling eyes.

. Paul introduced them and Michael took her hand and held it in a friendly grip. 'I'm absolutely delighted. I've been on at this man to settle down for a long time, haven't I, Paul? No blessing on this earth like a good wife.' It was said quizzically, with a humorous grin, but Kate heard the sincerity beneath. As she got into the car and Paul took his place beside her at the wheel she thought that Laura Nichols must be rather special and looked forward to meeting her.

It would be pleasant and reassuring to have a woman acquaintance in Hong Kong, while Paul was busy with his business affairs. She was prepared to like Laura.

As they drove smoothly along the wide, curving, intersecting freeways Paul was completely silent, but Michael leaned forward between them from the back seat, making pleasant small talk with Kate, enquiring after her journey and what the weather was like back at home, and pointing out places of interest. 'That's the entrance to the tunnel, the way you'd come in. The yacht club's down that way—we must see if we can get you some sailing while you're here. We're coming into the Wanchai district now—see all the neon lights down on the harbour?'

Kate caught glimpses of enormous neon signs, appearing and disappearing behind the buildings, running and switching and winking in every colour of the rainbow. 'It looks like a super Piccadilly Circus, back in London,' she laughed, and Michael retorted that Hong Kong would be extremely insulted if you compared its neon display to anything as down-market as Piccadilly Circus.

They were both enjoying the joke when Paul spoke for the first time, cutting in somewhat brusquely with, 'You didn't say where we're meeting the others, Mike.'

'Oh—sorry! Laura and I thought Lindy's might be a good place to eat, and make Howard and Max feel at home—you know, the old New York Lindy's.' He added to Kate, 'We have two friends from the U.S. staying with us, Howard and Max Stenz. Father and son—charming folk. Have you met them, Paul?'

Paul said no, he hadn't, and again Kate got the

impression that he was somewhat curt, but perhaps that was because they had left the freeway now and passed into what was evidently the main shopping part of Hong Kong, with huge whitely-lit shop windows lining both sides of the street of towering buildings, and the traffic was getting thick and congested.

'Lindy's?' Paul rapped out. 'Don't know it, you'll have to guide me.' Then, as if he realised that he was being somewhat less than polite to his dinner host, he added, 'I'm not well up on all the special dives in these parts, you know, not like you old residents. I'm only temporary.'

Michael said amiably, 'Sorry, Paul. It's in Wyndham Street, off Queen's Road—go straight along and I'll tell you.'

Soon the car pulled up. Paul glowered at the moving chaos of traffic round him and said, 'You'd better take Kate in, Mike, while I try to find somewhere to park. It'll probably take me some time.'

Kate thought it all looked splendidly Eastern and exotic, like a tunnel of dazzling lights and colours carved out of the tall dark buildings and the narrow strip of black velvet sky above. The neon signs made a blazing splurge of gaudy reds and yellows and greens all in their flowering of Chinese characters, and the wide shop windows and hotel entrances glittered with light.

She stole a look at Paul's profile as Michael helped her out of the car, and her heart sank. Paul looked hard and angry as she had seen him that first day in London. She wondered why. It couldn't merely be because he was going to find it difficult to park the car, surely?

Michael Nichols took her arm as the car drew

away, leading her to the turning into a narrow street off the main road, so steeply cut into the hill that it rose in steps. It seemed full of Chinese—men and women, young and old, and a good smattering of small children too—carrying a strange assortment of things—tins of petrol, heaps of washing, plastic flowers, some with panniers full of fish or vegetables, or bamboo baskets slung on either end of long poles resting across their shoulders. One woman had a baby in one basket, balanced by a load of cabbages in the other. And everywhere the street was thick with hanging signs and banners all with their gaudy painted symbols.

Kate was fascinated and would have stood there, drinking in the atmosphere of noise and colour and activity, but Michael, smiling at her enthusiasm, told her she would have plenty of time later to browse, and led her up more steps into the restaurant.

As they entered the well-appointed bar she noticed first the three people sitting at a corner table with drinks before them. The two men in the party stood up immediately they saw Michael and waited, smiling.

The woman wasn't smiling, she was staring at Kate as if she couldn't believe her eyes. What had Laura Nichols expected? Kate wondered. Had Paul's little-grey-mouse description reached as far as this, and didn't she fill the bill? But perhaps she had been mistaken about the surprise, for by the time they reached the table in the corner Laura was smiling in welcome and holding out her hand.

Her husband gave her an adoring glance and said, 'Darling, meet Paul's girl—this is Kate.

Kate—my wife, Laura.'

Kate's first impression of Laura was that Paul's word for her—spectacular—was an understatement. She was shattering. Vibrant dark red hair and the milk-white skin that so often goes with it; sea-green eyes which, now they had lost their first look of stunned surprise, sparkled with vivacity; a small perfect mouth with very even white teeth. She wore a jade trouser suit in dull satin that clung to her with explicit reference to a lovely body beneath. A pair of enormous gilt earrings shaped like sabres, so huge that their points reached to the base of her beautiful white neck, hung from delicate ears.

Crikey! breathed Kate to herself, resisting a giggle as she reminded herself how she had been eager to make a friend of Michael Nichols's wife. She had imagined someone as nice and unpretentious as Michael himself. Kate had never known a woman even remotely like Laura Nichols and in spite of all her good resolutions to be confident, she found herself feeling like a shy gauche teenager in the face of such supreme sophistication.

But Laura's smile was brilliant and very friendly as she held both Kate's hands. 'Hullo, Paul's girl.' Her voice was husky, with a ripple of mischief in it. 'Welcome to the wicked city of Hong Kong. Come and sit by me and tell Mike what you'll have to drink.' She glanced towards the door. 'And where have you left my adorable Paul, Mike?'

Her husband pulled a wry face. 'He's having a job to park his car, I'm afraid. We ought to have got a taxi, only I didn't think of it.'

Laura's mouth twisted. 'You wouldn't, would

you, darling?' she said sweetly. 'Now, be a good boy and get us all some more drinks.'

She issued her orders and Michael turned to the bar obediently. Laura pulled Kate down into a chair beside hers and smiled up at the two men, who were still standing politely. 'And now, Paul's girl, you must meet our friends from America. Howard Stenz——' she waved a graceful arm '—— and Max. When they're not keeping the world of big business ticking over in New York they breed horses in the wide open spaces. And——'. her voice mimicked an American drawl and she laid a hand caressingly on the sleeve of the elder man, who was standing nearest to her '—and they're a couple of real nice guys.'

Howard Stenz was a big man; grizzled, huskily tough-looking, with piercing blue eyes. He bowed over Kate's hand. 'De-lighted to meet you, ma'am.'

His son was definitely a good-looker. Early twenties, Kate judged, with thick shortish blond hair and the same clear blue eyes as his father. He had an eager, lively expression, as if he were expecting life to be fun, and as he took Kate's hand in his and held it, he looked into her eyes with undisguised admiration and said sincerely, 'I'm sure glad to know you, Kate.'

Michael came back with the drinks, everyone sat down and the talk became the casual talk of people who are just getting to know each other. Kate would have liked to stay in the background, feeling her way with these strangers, but Laura drew her into the conversation in an easy, friendly way and soon she found herself explaining to the Americans about the wild ponies on Dartmoor, near her home in Devon.

She was facing the doorway and saw Paul the moment he came in, and the sudden sight of him as he stood looking round the room, his dark lashes veiling his eyes, gave her an odd tingling deep inside that was almost like pain. It was the same feeling that she had had when she had seen him coming towards her in the hotel just now. What was it? Fear? Foreboding? Selfconsciousness? She didn't know why this man had this effect on her. She only knew that she seemed to be drawn towards him by a powerful magnet.

Laura's green eyes glittered as Paul approached their table. 'Well, well, look who we have here!' she cried gaily. 'Come and join the party.'

Her tone was the playful, intimate tone of an old friend, but he greeted her quite formally, as his hostess. 'Hullo, Laura, sorry I'm late. I hope I haven't held you up. I had a brute of a job parking the car.'

'Where did you manage to get in finally?' Michael enquired, on his way back to the bar.

Paul looked mock-guilty. 'I don't think I'd better confess, I might get hauled in by the police if it got around.'

'Dar-*ling*!' drawled Laura delightedly. 'You're so beautifully resourceful, Paul. Now if it had been Michael he'd have walked miles before he'd do anything illegal.' She wrinkled her nose towards her husband's disappearing back.

Paul gave her a cool glance. 'Oh, it wasn't really illegal. I don't go in for breaking the rules.'

Laura's eyebrows slid upwards. 'No?' she said provocatively. 'I suppose it all depends which rules we're talking about.'

There was a sudden little silence. Kate saw the way Paul's dark brows drew together into a frown. She was beginning to recognise that frown by now. He didn't like being needled.

Michael came back with Paul's drink and introduced him to the two Americans. Then Paul pulled up a chair between Laura and Kate and took Kate's hand lovingly in his. 'Okay, sweetheart?' His tone, his look, were just right for a newly-engaged man. She smiled back at him, nodding, and feeling—of all unexpected emotions—ridiculously shy.

Laura touched Paul's arm lightly. 'Paul dear, you've been so clever to find yourself such a pretty girl. Your Kate is quite charming and I mean to see a lot of her and give her a good time while she's here. You and Mike are always so disgustingly busy in the daytime, but we'll look after Katy for you, won't we, boys?' she appealed merrily to the two Americans.

Howard Stenz gave his hearty laugh. 'We surely will, if the young lady agrees, won't we, Max?'

His son's eyes were fixed intently on Kate. 'Surely,' he echoed enthusiastically.

Laura's green eyes slid towards Paul. 'Don't look so peeved, Paul sweetie, if you'll lend her to us in the daytime you can have her all to yourself at night.'

The suggestion was so crude and so obvious that Kate felt her cheeks flame crimson. Michael looked across the table and murmured, 'Laura—really!' and Laura clapped a hand to her mouth. 'Goodness, what did I say, how awful of me! I talk too much, that's my trouble. So sorry, darlings, it was meant quite innocently.'

She leaned across Paul towards Kate. 'You'll forgive me, won't you, my dear, and let us show you the sights?' Her smile was warm now, her voice sincerely apologetic, but Kate hesitated, feeling vastly uncomfortable. She thought she could feel a tension between Paul and the woman on his other side. What was their relationship to each other? she wondered uneasily.

She felt Paul's hand tighten over hers, crushing her fingers until they hurt. A warning? She murmured noncommittally, 'Thank you, it's very kind of you, Mrs Nichols.'

Laura clapped her hands delightedly. 'Splendid! Now I know I'm forgiven for making that stupid gaffe. We'll fix up a really interesting, exciting itinerary. Howard and Max are just crazy to see the sights of Hong Kong. We'll have some splendid excursions while Paul and Mike are stuck in their stuffy offices, won't we, Katy?' Her voice became warm as she added, 'And you must *please* call me Laura.'

It was a relief when the waiter came to announce that their table was ready and they moved into the restaurant.

Kate found it impossible to relax over dinner—an American-style meal. 'We'll show you Chinese food another time,' Michael told Kate. 'This is a compliment to our two American friends who are known to be very choosy about their steaks.'

He grinned goodhumouredly across the table at Howard Stenz and his son, and Howard grinned back, 'Now I call that real friendly, Mike.'

The dinner proceeded on the level of lighthearted talk and chaff. Kate recognised that the steaks were out of this world—thick and luscious and more tender than any steak she had ever tasted before, but even so she could only manage about half of what was on her plate. It was easier to enjoy the angel cake that followed—it literally melted in her mouth, a dream dessert. They drank a red wine, which she found made her feel rather muzzy, and on top of that the strain of all the travelling was really beginning to take its toll now.

Fortunately nobody seemed to expect her to talk. Howard Stenz did most of that, telling stories of his ranch and anecdotes about the buying and selling of his horses, and Kate was able to fix a smile on her lips and let her attention wander. Inevitably it centred upon the man sitting next to her. To her dismay she found herself almost painfully conscious of Paul's nearness. When he leaned closer to attend to her wants her inside contracted sharply and her heart pounded. Her awareness of him was so keen that she thought, in dismay, that he must sense it himself.

But if he did he showed no sign of it. He was quiet, courteous, a little withdrawn perhaps, but joining in the conversation round the table pleasantly at times, at other times listening with apparent interest. The perfect guest, thought Kate rather sourly, as he was the perfect everything else—*and* he knew it!

Towards the end of the meal Michael became a little formal and raised his glass, saying seriously, 'And now it's my real pleasure to welcome Kate among us and to hope that she will have a most enjoyable stay in Hong Kong. I'm sure you'll all join me in wishing her and Paul every joy and many, many years of happiness together.'

Kate felt as if the smile were freezing on her lips. She felt dreadful. Michael was such a nice, sincere person and it seemed awful that he should be deceived. Paul ought to feel the same—

Michael was his friend—but he didn't seem in the least aware of it. He smiled his dark-lashed, controlled smile and put an arm round Kate's shoulders, drawing her closer to him. 'Thanks, Mike, from both of us. For myself, I'm well aware of my incredible luck.'

He turned his smile full on her and then bent his head to kiss her softly. There was laughter round the table and a little burst of clapping, in which some of the diners at the other tables, guessing what was going on, joined in. Below the ripple of sound and the clink of glasses Kate heard Laura Nichols, on Paul's other side, exclaim in her husky amused voice, 'How touching! We only need the violins to play.' And then, when the clapping had subsided, she added gaily, 'Now let's do some more celebrating. How about going on to a night spot to dance? What do you feel about that, Howard?' She put a hand lingeringly on the big American's arm.

Paul's dark head was very close to Kate's and she could still feel the warm disturbing touch of his lips on hers. He said under his breath, 'Do you want to go on anywhere?'

She shook her head slightly. She had never been to a 'night spot' in her life, but she guessed that a night spot in Hong Kong would be more hectic than in most other places—more noisy, more colourful, in a higher key. The last thing she needed at this moment was an excess of brittle gaiety; she just wanted to lay her head on a cool pillow and drift off to sleep. 'Oh, no, please,' she whispered.

She heard him murmur 'Good,' and then he raised his voice to say that Kate had had a long day and although she seemed amazingly immune to jet-lag, he thought it better for her to have a good night's rest and that if Mike and Laura would forgive them they would take their leave. He stood up and drew Kate to her feet while he was speaking, and as his arm closed round her protectively she could almost have laughed aloud. It was so very typical of Paul. Once he had made up his mind to do something, he was right there in the middle of the action.

Three minutes later they had said goodnight to Michael and Laura, with suitable thanks for the party, shaken hands with the two Americans, and were outside in the brilliant dazzle of the street.

'My word, that was quick,' Kate commented. 'You don't waste time, do you?'

She heard his deep chuckle. 'I long ago learned not to linger when you reach the end of any-thing—and we'd reached the end of that par-ticular party.' He tucked her arm through his as they made their way along the thronged pave-ments. After the cool inside the restaurant, the air was hot and humid and again Kate longed for her air-conditioned room at the hotel. She felt her body sag a little against Paul's.

He stopped and looked down at her. 'You really are fagged out, aren't you? We shouldn't have gone to that bloody dinner,' he said in his angry voice.

'I'm okay,' she began, but he wasn't listening. He was moving away from her, dodging round a tall trolleybus, avoiding another coming from behind as he made a risky dive to the opposite side of the road. She saw a red car with a silvery top come to a sudden stop, and then Paul was beside her again.

'I just spotted a taxi,' he said. 'Come on, we'll get you back in no time.'

'But your car——' she began as he steered her towards the waiting taxi. 'You can't leave it behind.'

'No problem—I'll collect it later.' The Chinese driver was beaming widely, holding the door open for her, and she shrugged and got in.

Paul climbed in after her and slammed the door and as the taxi eased its way into the steady mass of traffic he put an arm around her and drew her head down against his shoulder. 'Relax, sweetheart,' he told her. 'The worst's over and you did very well. I was proud of my new fiancée.'

Kate yawned. She really was very tired and it was heavenly to feel the warmth and solidity of him so close. It seemed the most natural thing in the world to snuggle even closer and when he dropped his cheek against the top of her smooth head she closed her eyes and sank into a half-sleep.

Soon the brightness of the lights coming and going against her eyelids became dimmer and she realised they must have left the central part of the city and reached the freeway. She opened her eyes and raised her head a little and found Paul's face only inches away from hers.

In the darkness of the car they looked at each other. Then Paul moved. His other hand came up and slipped behind her neck, burying itself in her hair and he drew her mouth towards his, their lips meeting in a long, close kiss which Kate couldn't have resisted even if she had wanted to.

The kiss became deeper, the first tenderness changing to a flaring passion and she could feel his body start to tremble against hers. Her own body wakened and responded, a treacherous weakness beginning to seep all through her as her arm found its way beneath the thin stuff of his white jacket and pressed against the firm muscular strength of his back, warm and pulsing with vitality through the silk shirt.

When, abruptly, he drew away from her it was almost like a physical pain. She saw that the taxi was turning into the forecourt of her hotel and straightened up, putting a shaking hand to her hair. In the brilliant light streaming out from the entrance she watched Paul paying the driver; then the door was opened and he was holding a hand to help her out.

But as soon as she had got out he let go of her hand immediately, and they walked into the hotel in silence, a little way apart. Paul turned towards the reception desks. 'I'll get the key—what's your room number?'

The brightly-lit foyer, the people, the sound of voices, the scent of flowers and the green of the feathery palms, seemed to Kate like something out of a dream. They were whisked up in the express lift and in a few moments Paul had fitted the key to her bedroom door and they were inside.

What now? Her brain, tired with the hectic stimulation of all that had happened since that wet day in London, less than two weeks ago, refused to work. Her body longed for rest and the cool feel of the pillow beneath her head. And yet, with a sensuous weakness, it longed too for the comfort and intoxicating pleasure of being in Paul's arms again.

She sank down on the side of the bed and put a

hand to her forehead, as if she could push back the chaotic thoughts that were seething behind it.

Paul stood looking round the room with a critical eye. 'H'm, not bad! The Victorian decor would be up-to-the-minute back at home, wouldn't it? I thought you'd be happier here than in one of the more trendy new hotels.' The dark eyes danced. 'That was, of course, when I expected a little grey church mouse.'

Kate closed her eyes. She didn't want to go into all *that* again.

'But you aren't a mouse, of course. You're a modern, confident, consciously disturbing young woman.'

'Am I?' whispered Kate. Was that how he saw her? She hardly recognised herself at this moment.

He was prowling round the room now, and stopped before the mini-bar. 'You're well supplied with drinks,' he said. 'What will you have?'

She opened her eyes. 'Something long and cool, please. Definitely nothing alcoholic.' She had to try to clear her head and keep it clear. The next few minutes were absolutely crucial. So far, Paul had only hinted at his intentions, but if he went further and brought all the pressure of his charisma and expertise in lovemaking to bear on her, in her hazy state, she knew she wouldn't be able to resist.

And she *had* to resist, she thought desperately. To enter into an affair with Paul Caister would be utter folly. To him it would just be a game, an extension of the game they were playing already. But for her—if she let him make love to her the game would end and turn into a nightmare of longing for something he couldn't give her. He would only want a girl to sleep with; she would want more—so much more.

He held up a bottle. 'Tonic water?'

'That sounds very appropriate.' She grinned faintly.

He filled two glasses and came and sat beside her on the bed. He raised his glass. 'To us—and our engagement!' A smile lurked behind the long dark lashes.

Kate didn't respond. She tossed off her drink and the cool bitterness of it revived her a little. She moved slightly away from him to put the glass down on the locker beside the bed. Then she yawned, letting out her breath on a long sigh. 'Ooh, I'm so tired.'

The springs of the big bed creaked slightly as he leaned across her to put his own glass down. '*Very* tired?' he said softly. His hand closed over hers, sliding up her bare arm to her shoulder, very slowly, finding its way behind her neck to close on the other shoulder, drawing her gently against him. '*Very* tired?' he murmured again into her ear, as his mouth pushed her hair aside to come to rest against her temple.

Every nerve in her body leaped in response and she was floating in a warm sea of sensual feeling, beyond knowing or caring now what happened. His mouth left her temple and trailed down her cheekbone to brush against her own mouth, finding it in a long kiss that sent tongues of fire licking through her. The tiredness had turned to a drugging sweetness now, rendering her quite helpless to resist whatever it was he wanted from her. The hunger that had begun out there in the darkness of the taxi was drawing her inevitably towards its satisfaction. Paul lifted her legs on to the bed and she felt his weight as he lowered himself beside her, his arm imprisoning her strongly.

The sound of the telephone burred through her head like a physical pain and she heard Paul mutter a colourful oath as she stretched out an arm to take the instrument off its cradle.

Laura's amused voice came from the other end of the line. 'Kate? I'd calculated you would be back at your hotel by now. I do hope I'm not interrupting anything.' A significant pause and Kate could almost see the green eyes narrowing mischievously. When there was no reply she went on quickly, 'It was so lovely to meet you, Katy, and I thought we might fix something up for tomorrow morning. Michael says that he and Paul will be attending a meeting, so you could come along with us. I'm showing Howard and Max round a bit and we thought we might go to the first race meeting in the afternoon. How about it?'

Kate's head was spinning. 'Tomorrow morning? It's very kind of you, but I'm not sure——'

Paul's head was close to hers and she knew he must have heard every word that Laura spoke. He swung his legs off the bed and took the receiver from Kate's hand in one abrupt movement.

'Laura? Yes, of course I'm here . . . well, what did you expect? . . . no, I'm damn well not . . . I'll be leaving for my own apartment when I've seen that Kate is comfortable . . . all right, my dear, think what you like . . .'

There was a pause. Kate could hear the murmur of Laura's voice but not the words. Paul's mouth was set in a grim line as he listened.

At last he said definitely, 'No. Sorry, Laura,

but Kate is spending tomorrow with me. No, I've arranged with Michael about the meeting. All right, my dear, ask him if you don't believe me.' He held the receiver a little away from his ear. 'Thanks for the dinner, Laura, and we'll be seeing you. Good-*night*.'

He replaced the phone with a little thump, his eyes on Kate, who had raised herself on one elbow, her eyes bright, her pale-gold hair dishevelled.

'Well, that's put an end to *that* tender little interlude,' he said furiously. 'Nothing so calculated to spoil the atmosphere as a telephone! Blast the woman, I might have known.'

Known what? Kate wondered dazedly. Oh well, it didn't matter. As he so crudely put it, the atmosphere had been spoiled, and just as well that it had. She had been betrayed by fatigue, too much red wine, and the practised charm of a man to whom a love affair was just a temporary diversion. Or perhaps she was merely a stand-in for Gabrielle, the girl whom he had been— probably still was—crazy about? Perhaps he would have taken her in his arms and tried to believe that Gabrielle was there instead. The thought sickened her.

She sat up and pushed back her hair. 'Will you go now, please?' she said quietly.

He stood beside the bed, looking down at her with a faint frown. Then he shrugged. 'Okay, I'll go. I'll call you in the morning and we'll go out somewhere. It's time we got to know each other.' He walked to the door and turned. 'I'll tell them to send breakfast up to you. Goodnight, Kate. Sleep well.'

She lay and stared at the closed door. She

ought to hate him—and despise him. She *did* hate and despise him, she told herself. It had been the luckiest moment of her life when the telephone rang just now. She would have to take the greatest care not to let herself get into a situation like that again.

She dragged herself off the bed and began to undress. It was just the tiredness, she assured herself, that was making her feel so flat and so dejected.

CHAPTER FIVE

KATE had expected to sleep until all hours next morning, but surprisingly she was awake soon after seven, and immediately all the happenings of the previous evening became vividly clear in her mind, which made it quite impossible to settle down and try to sleep again.

She had no idea what time her breakfast would arrive and she hadn't the confidence to ring the room service bell to find out. Neither could she just lie in bed and wait—and think. In the end she was showered, and dressed in one of the classic little numbers Polly had chosen for her—a crisp, silver-grey cotton with white geometrical design and a white bow collar—when there was a tap at the door and she opened it to find a smiling Chinese waiter outside with a tray.

'Oh, thank you. Please put it on the table over by the window.'

She gestured, wondering if he spoke English. He evidently understood, for he did as she asked and then stood beaming and nodding. 'Okay? Everything okay?' His voice had a high Chinese lilt to it.

Kate beamed back. 'Yes. Everything is fine, thank you.' She found herself nodding too. He looked so cheerful and happy, this young man in his waiter's uniform of dark trousers and red jacket with the silver buttons—as if he really cared whether she was satisfied or not.

She found herself still smiling as she sat down

to tackle the crisp rolls and coffee and fresh melon, but by the time she was drinking her last cup of coffee tremors of nervousness began to assail her every time her eye caught the telephone.

What time would Paul ring her? He hadn't said. All he had said was 'I'll call you in the morning.' That might be any time. She mustn't—she must *not*—allow herself to get jittery every time she was due to contact him; that was too absurd for words. She would put him out of her mind altogether until the phone actually rang, and even then she wouldn't hurry to answer. She would let him wait.

The phone buzzed as she was finishing the last drops in her cup and she started violently. The cup clattered into its saucer, brown liquid draining out. Kate stumbled across the room and almost fell on to the bed, grabbing the receiver with nerveless fingers.

'Kate? Good morning, did you sleep well?'

His voice, deep and velvety even coming across a telephone wire, did terrible things to her inside. 'Y-yes, thank you,' she gulped.

'Good—fine. Let's make some arrangements, then. How soon can you be ready?'

'I—I'm ready now—any time.'

'You're dressed—breakfasted?' He sounded amazed.

'Yes.' It occurred to her that he would be accustomed to his women emerging from their rooms around midday, probably, after sophisticated parties that ended at dawn. She could imagine Laura Nichols doing just that.

'Incredible!' He still sounded as if he couldn't believe it. 'Well then, I'll come and pick you up

in a few minutes and we'll drive into the Central
District first. I have to call in at the office briefly
and then the rest of the day will be our own. In
ten minutes' time—in the lobby downstairs—
okay?'

'Okay,' said Kate faintly, and hung up.

It was agony, but she forced herself to wait for
a quarter of an hour before she went down to the
lobby. Slowly and deliberately she gave in her
key at Reception and then strolled across to the
entrance, looking around her at the morning activities of the staff, of the young Chinese waiters in
their red coats, who seemed to be busy everywhere, always smiling and nodding at guests. She
fastened her gaze on the huge hanging light fittings, in the shape of lanterns, and caught
glimpses of what looked like a coffee lounge on a
balcony above. She looked everywhere but at the
entrance doors, where Paul might be waiting for
her. She would certainly not rush stupidly into
his arms as she had done yesterday evening.

'Hullo, Kate.' His voice, coming from behind,
stopped her in her tracks, the colour flooding into
her cheeks.

She spun round, her breath catching in her
throat, and looked up at him standing there, big
and handsome in casual clothes—jeans and a dark
brown shirt, open at the neck—with a faint smile
hovering round his mouth and a quizzical look in
his eyes. Her heart seemed to flip up and turn
right over and she thought, Oh God, it's no good.
I'm in love with the man. I'm crazy about him,
and there's no way of stopping it or pretending to
myself that I'm not. But she must never let him
know, she thought desperately. She must go on
pretending it was as much a game to her as it was

to him.

His arm went round her lightly and he dropped a brief kiss on her forehead. 'You're looking very charming this morning, Kate. That silver grey colour suits you. It matches your eyes.'

She glanced at him under her lashes as they walked towards the entrance door, guarded by the huge, colourful Sikh in his white turban. 'Thank you,' she said demurely. 'You look very fetching yourself.'

She heard his deep chuckle. 'For a lovers' greeting that wasn't too bad! We're making progress.'

His white car was standing outside. As Kate climbed in she began, 'You managed to——' and stopped. She had been going to say, 'You managed to get your car back last night, then?' But the memory of last night set her inside churning, so she substituted somewhat lamely, 'You managed to get here very quickly.'

He got into the seat beside her and turned deliberately to meet her eyes, one hand on the starting key. 'Oh yes, I had the car at my apartment. I trekked back into town to retrieve it last night after I left you.'

The dark eyes held hers, and there was a wicked glint in them. If she wanted to forget last night he certainly didn't, and he was showing her that he didn't.

They drove quickly along the freeway, more laboriously through the teeming streets of Wanchai and ended up, just short of Central District, in a colossal traffic jam. Paul didn't fret or fluster. He switched off his engine and waited, quite unperturbed, until they could get through. 'This usually happens,' he said. 'I hope you're not too hot.'

Once again his thoughtfulness shook her. It seemed so out of character that he should care whether she was comfortable or not—and yet something in his tone seemed to imply that he did. The way he said it was—caressing. She shivered as if he had touched her.

When they at last got through the traffic to the Barn Trekker Office in one of the soaring modern blocks overlooking the harbour, Paul parked the car and asked, 'Will you be okay here for a few minutes, or would you like to come inside?'

Kate said she would stay in the car. It was very hot, but it would be even more trying to spend a few minutes in a cool air-conditioned building and then have to come out again.

She sat looking about her. The constant coming and going of people fascinated her. Here in the business quarter there were many young Chinese men in their lightweight suits and neat hair-do's; not so very different, except in colouring, from their counterparts in London. There were older men here and there, shabbily dressed in cotton trousers and flapping shirts, moving slowly in their odd, shuffling walk. The older women too seemed weighed down by the cares of life, carrying heavy bundles. Children were everywhere, running and playing and climbing. Beyond the road, the harbour was busy with craft of every shape and size, from small rowing boats to a huge ocean liner, white and beautiful, which appeared to be moving out from its berth on the mainland side of the harbour.

'Hullo, Miss Reynolds—Kate.'

She turned her head to see Josh Kinney, Paul's P.A., standing beside the open car window, his pleasant freckled face beaming with pleasure. 'Nice to see you again. How are you enjoying H.K.?'

She smiled at him. 'Hullo, Josh. Give me a chance, I haven't been here a whole day yet! But I'm fascinated by what I've seen so far—all the noise and colour and frenzied activity. Sometimes it's too much—we got stuck in a traffic jam just now and I thought we'd never get here.' She pointed across the harbour. 'I've been watching that lovely ship over there.'

Josh told her it was a cruise liner leaving the Ocean Terminal on the mainland of Kowloon opposite. He lingered by the car, leaning in at the open window, pointing out the various piers and ferries to her, while she sat back and listened, amused. Josh looked as if he would like to stay here all morning, chatting.

'You should get Paul to take you to Macau while you're here. It's a really romantic spot. You can have a flutter at the tables and eat gorgeous seafood and browse among tropical flowers and lie on the beach under the banyan trees— heavenly! I'd like to take you there myself, only I'd be so lucky.' He pulled a comically wry face. 'Paul would push my face in if he could read my mind.'

Kate burst out laughing. He was fun, this young man with the saucy grin and the thatch of red hair, and she half wished she could actually have a day out with him. It would be a light-hearted affair, not at all like her relationship with Paul, which seemed to have a charge of dynamite built into it, liable to explode at any moment.

But Josh Kinney was more like the young men she had gone out with when she worked in a soli-

citor's office in Torquay. She had never in her
life encountered a man like Paul Caister. Even
Mr Charles, her somewhat formidable boss, was
considerably less formidable than Paul.

Josh's back was turned to the office building,
but Kate saw Paul come out. Saw, too, the way
his face darkened when he spied Josh leaning in at
the car window, his red head close to Kate's as
they laughed together. The laughter died on
Josh's lips as Paul came up to the car and he
straightened up immediately. 'I've been over to
the bank—I was just coming up to the office.'

Paul eyed the young man for a devastating
moment in silence, then he said dryly, 'Really?
Shouldn't you be on your way, then?'

'Yes, yes, of course. Well then—au revoir,
Miss Reynolds, nice to have seen you again,' Josh
gabbled, and departed towards the office at a
brisk trot.

Paul got into the car and sat for a moment
looking straight ahead. Then he said stiffly, 'I'd
prefer it, Kate, if you didn't find it necessary to
flirt with the members of staff. It gives a wrong
impression.'

She had felt hot before, but now she boiled.
'Really! How pompous can you get? I certainly
wasn't flirting, the whole idea's simply ridiculous!' She looked at the hard impassive face of the
man beside her and would dearly like to have
slapped it. 'Surely I can talk to who I like without asking your permission. Or is that included in
your—your beastly blackmailing contract too—
that I'm completely at your command?'

He turned his head and looked at her and she
saw to her chagrin that an odd, satisfied kind of
smile lurked round his thin mouth. 'Calm down,

Kate, you *have* lost your cool, haven't you? Don't take it so personally, that's a good girl. Now, if you don't mind walking a short way we'll go and get the business side of our agreement settled. I'll open an account in your name at my bank here. You'll need money and it's not a good idea to carry too much of it about with you. The Chinese are great on upping the price of anything if they can spot a gullible, soft-hearted customer, and I shan't always be at hand to bargain for you.'

'Oh!' snapped Kate, her cheeks pink with rage, 'so I'm stupid and gullible now, am I, as well as silly and flirtatious?'

He laughed aloud—a rare happening. 'You're rather sweet,' he said lightly. 'Come along, let's get the dull part over, then we'll have a long cool drink and decide what to do next.' He might have been speaking to a child, Kate thought, prickling with annoyance. What a maddening individual he was—you never knew where you stood with him for two minutes at a time.

But the idea of a long cool drink sounded wonderful, so she got out of the car when he held the door open for her, but carefully avoided taking the hand he held out. So long as he didn't touch her she could keep up the pretence that she was indifferent to the masculine charisma that he had flaunted since she arrived in Hong Kong. As they walked through the busy streets to the bank she remembered how Polly had said, '*Make* him notice you. What have you got to lose?' and how they had laughed together about it.

It seemed that she had succeeded, in part at least. He was certainly noticing her. The trouble was that now she realised, as she hadn't done when she laughed so merrily about it with Polly, that she had a great deal to lose. Pretty well everything, in fact.

Half an hour later they were back at the car. Kate had a brand new cheque book tucked away in her handbag and was feeling cool and composed after a delicious long iced drink with fruit floating on the top.

'Now then, what next?' Paul mused, getting in behind the wheel. 'I had thought of a drive out into the New Territories, to get the tourists' obligatory look at the border with Communist China, but it's much too hot for that. I think the most comfortable spot is on the water today—what do you say? We could go native and hire a wallah-wallah complete with boatman, but I prefer to handle a craft myself, when I can. Mike has a small motorboat berthed at the yacht club—he lets me use her any time.' He started the engine and headed the big white car back the way they had come. 'Yes, that's what we'll do,' he said decisively.

Kate smiled to herself. When Paul Caister spoke in that tone you didn't argue with him. Not that she wanted to argue, and when, some time later, she was sitting beside him in the stern of Mike Nichols's smart little motor dinghy as they skimmed over the calm blue-grey waters of the harbour, she thought there could be no nicer way of spending a very hot day.

'We'll have a look at the New Territories from the water side,' he said. 'Then we'll thread our way between the islands and put in at Cheung Chau Island, which is one of the larger ones. You get the real Chinese flavour there without the crush of Hong Kong or Kowloon.' He grinned. 'If you're a good girl I'll show you a pirate cave.

Anyway, we can get some lunch there, find somewhere pleasant to laze for a while and then make the round trip back to Hong Kong.'

Afterwards, Kate was to remember that nothing happened to mar the pleasure of that trip. Nothing, that was, until the very end of it. But she had no premonition of that as they headed across the harbour, making for the opposite coastline, as Paul pointed out landmarks and gave her snippets of information he had picked up during his earlier stay in Hong Kong.

He was quite obviously making an effort to entertain her and be an amusing companion. At first she found herself wondering why he bothered. Did he think he owed it to her for having persuaded—forced!—her to come out here and put herself in a somewhat false position? Or was he—she shied away from the thought—deliberately trying to charm her and soften her up for a big seduction scene later?

She refused to let herself dwell on that, enjoying the passing moments of delight, feeling the air moving coolly over her cheeks, watching the way the little boat lifted its prow out of the water eagerly as Paul increased speed once they were away from the main shipping in the harbour.

'It's heavenly!' Her eyes sparkled, her cheeks were flushed with the exhilaration of the moment. 'Thank you for bringing me.'

She smiled up at him almost shyly and thought how devastating he looked, his hair blown by the breeze, his eyes dark smudges against the brown of his cheeks, his arm showing strong muscles where he had rolled up his shirt sleeves as his hand rested on the controls.

He turned his head and smiled back at her and

she thought her heart would stop beating. 'My pleasure,' he said, and with his free arm he drew her against him and repeated, close to her ear, 'My very great pleasure.' She thought he dropped a kiss on her hair before he raised his head, but she couldn't be sure because her senses were spinning wildly.

It was a golden day. Cheung Chau Island, as he had said, seemed almost entirely Chinese with its crowded lanes of small shops, flimsy-looking balconies where the inevitable lines and poles full of washing hung out, gaudy banners and shop signs in splashy reds and yellows. Everywhere noise and people and colour. Everything decorated with the twisty Chinese lettering that seemed to Kate to be pictures in themselves.

'Can you read them?' she asked Paul, but he shook his head and said he had learned a little Cantonese—the principal of the many Chinese dialects spoken in Hong Kong—but not to read the characters.

'Let's be tourists,' he said, and put an arm around her, and they strolled along among the passing crowds of people, pausing to look into the dark little caverns of shops selling everything imaginable, from clothing and household ware, fish, meat, fancy bits and pieces of every kind—pens, lighters, ornaments, cheap jewellery, books and records. There were jade pieces too, which Paul viewed with the deepest suspicion, saying he'd like an expert's opinion before he risked his good money. But he said it with a laugh—they laughed together a lot—and he relented by entering the little shop and buying a large paper fan decorated with a red dragon, which he presented ceremoniously to Kate.

They found a small, very clean, restaurant and lunched off a selection of seafood dishes in mysterious and delicious sauces, with sweet corn and bean sprouts and other succulent items that Kate didn't recognise, served in ornamental small side dishes. She found the long yellow chopsticks tricky to handle at first and was thankful for the small napkins soaked in perfumed water which the Chinese waiter handed to her as a matter of course.

She saw Paul's dark eyes dancing with amusement and grumbled, 'It's all very well for you to laugh. You seem to manage these peculiar instruments very cleverly, do you practise much?'

He laughed. 'I was as ham-handed as you, my child, when I first came out here, but I've had several visits in the last eight or nine months and I'm getting the knack now.'

She chased a prawn round her bowl and finally captured it. 'This is your final term here, is it?' she asked casually. She must at all costs keep everything casual, and not spoil the atmosphere of this enchanted day.

'Almost certainly,' he said. 'The new branch here is firmly on its feet now and won't need my services much longer. It may even be less than a month, I can't say yet. Anyway, I'm due in the U.S. in November and I want to have some time at home before I leave.'

'At your cottage in Devon?'

He gave her a wicked look, the long dark lashes lowered over his eyes. 'That's right—our holiday there together, remember?'

Last time he said that she had been angry, angry that he seemed to be taking it for granted that she would fall in with his wishes if he suggested an affair. This time it was just fooling, of course, but there was something infinitely more dangerous in the foolery. Something intimate. Something that lay between them, deep and un-acknowledged. At least that was how it seemed to her, but she could be wrong. It could be simply wishful thinking. It could be just part of the game they were playing.

She laughed lightly. 'The answer's still no,' she said.

Paul lifted his bowl of jasmine tea to his lips, meeting her eyes over the rim. 'We'll have to see what we can do about that,' he said darkly, and she felt her heart sink abysmally. Yes, it was all part of the game, so why kid herself that he was being even part-way serious?

When they emerged from the restaurant it was hotter than ever, the air full of water vapour so that your clothes clung to you uncomfortably. Sightseeing was out of the question, even moving was an effort. They found a quiet spot on the beach, shaded by overhanging shrubby trees with enormous leaves, and stretched out on the warm sand.

Paul lay back and closed his eyes. 'Sorry about the pirates' cave,' he murmured. 'Another time, perhaps.'

Kate took out a handkerchief and mopped her forehead. 'Is it always as hot as this?'

He shook his head. 'We're just at the change-over of the seasons. In the summer it's hot and there's a lot of rain—typhoons too at times. In the winter, from October onwards it's still delight-fully warm but not so humid and there's very little rain.'

Kate said, 'We're not likely to get a typhoon,

are we?' She had only the vaguest idea what that would mean, but it sounded rather terrifying.

He squinted up at the sky. 'Shouldn't think so, it's rather late in the season for typhoons, but maybe we should be getting back as soon as we can drag ourselves to the boat.'

Kate would have enjoyed staying where she was, just stretched out in the shade, but now Paul seemed anxious to get back. 'You shouldn't have put the idea of typhoons into my mind,' he teased, pulling her to her feet. 'I shan't be happy until we've crossed the harbour.' He grinned and added, 'I feel responsible for you, you know. I intend to hand you back to your loving family in good order.'

She released her hands from his. 'When I've served my purpose?'

He stood looking at her in silence for a long moment. Then he said enigmatically, 'Quite.'

She stumbled after him across the sand and in spite of the heat it was as if a chill ran over her body.

On the trip back Kate followed their progress on the map of Hong Kong provided by the management of her hotel, and marvelled at the number of islands that sprinkled the sea. Most of them were without water and uninhabited, Paul told her, and even Hong Kong Island itself had once been an almost barren rock until it was acquired for Queen Victoria, and the British started on a long programme of cultivation and reclaiming land from the sea.

Kate listened attentively, putting in questions now and then, fascinated by the amount of knowledge this man seemed to have of a country which, he said, he had only visited two or three

times during the past year—and never before
that. By the time they were back in the harbour
she felt she knew a little of the history of this
fascinating, overcrowded, colourful corner of the
world, which could still call itself British.

'You're a good listener,' Paul told her, and she
flushed with pleasure at his words, spoken without any of the ironic tone he usually adopted towards her. They seemed to put a seal on the sense
of companionship she had felt growing between
them all the afternoon. It probably didn't mean
much, but it was better than having him angry
and cynical.

They were almost back at their starting point—
the yacht club—when it happened. Kate had
been watching the manoeuvres of all the different
craft they were passing and had been most interested in the Chinese junks and sampans, where
washing hung out at every available place and the
smell of cooking wafted on the air. She was
amazed at the way the tiny, mostly naked, children ran and climbed about on the decks, apparently without fear. One of the sampans
seemed alive with their small, sunburned bodies,
twisting and somersaulting on the very edge of
the flattened end of the craft, which was composed of laths where fishing nets were spread out
and looped around wooden posts to dry. One tiny
child, not more than eighteen months or so, was
staggering and teetering precariously, but the
other children took no notice.

Kate's heart was in her mouth. 'Look, Paul,'
she cried, 'that baby's not safe there. It's going to
fall——'

Before she could finish the sentence, the worst
happened. One of the children slipped on the

netting, tried to save himself by clutching at the tiny one, who threw out its little arms, swayed horribly, and toppled over into the water.

Kate cried out, but there seemed no grown-up on the sampan to hear. The other children were squealing now, frightened. Paul, alerted in time to what had happened, cut out the engine and reached over the side, grabbing at the little naked body, but it slipped from his hands and sank under the water.

In a flash he tugged off his sandals and heaved himself over the side, leaving the boat rocking with the violence of his action. Kate put out both hands, trying to balance the boat, her eyes on the water where the baby had disappeared.

Everything happened with the speed of light, it seemed. Paul dived, to emerge a couple of moments later, holding a small brown body above the water. Kate's heart lifted with relief as she saw the baby wriggle; he was very much alive still.

A man had appeared on the sampan now, a very ancient man in flapping cotton trousers, smoking a long, thin-stemmed pipe, which he didn't remove from his mouth. Apparently unmoved, his weathered brown face a mass of crisscrossed wrinkles, he picked up the baby as Paul lifted it to him, and stood looking down into the water. Then, very slowly, the mouth that still held the pipe contorted into what might have been a grin, and he nodded his head up and down as he repeated one word, over and over. Then he turned away and shuffled out of sight under a primitive canvas awning at the back of the craft, the baby under his arm.

Paul hoisted himself back into the motorboat

and grinned as he pushed his dripping hair out of his eyes. He flopped down beside Kate, panting slightly. 'That,' he said, 'is what happens when you leave Grandpa to baby-sit.'

Kate laughed shakily. 'Are you all right?' He wouldn't want her to fuss, but she couldn't manage to keep her voice steady. When she had seen him go under the water just now she had had one of the worst moments of her life. Stupid really, because she should have guessed that he was a superb swimmer, but it had been what in modern jargon was known as a gut reaction and she couldn't stop it.

He squeezed the water from the bottom of his jeans and it dripped on the wooden boards making a little stream. 'Fine—fine. Not really dressed for deep sea diving, of course.'

He started up the motor and they glided away. 'I meant to take you to the hotel for real Chinese tea, but I think we'd better get back to my place first. I shouldn't imagine I'd be welcome in this costume at a restaurant, even when it's dried on me.' He wrinkled his nose. 'Did you know that Hong Kong means Fragrant Harbour? You could have fooled me!'

He was silent for a minute, his eyes on the water ahead, his hands on the controls, guiding the boat back to its berth. 'Funny little thing,' he mused. 'It was like trying to catch a slippery, wriggling small fish with your bare hands.'

Kate felt tears of reaction flood into her eyes. 'Oh, Paul—if we hadn't been there——'

'But we were,' he patted her hand briefly, 'so all's well.'

She nodded. 'At least the old man was grateful, though he didn't really look it. I suppose he was thanking you—did you understand what he said?'

He looked very grim. 'I can't say he was exactly thanking me. I know enough of the lingo to gather what he was telling me. He didn't have to tell me, though—I knew. There are plenty of 'em about in the harbour.'

Something in his face, in the way his mouth firmed into a straight line made Kate's inside jolt sickly. 'Plenty of—of what?'

'Sharks,' said Paul laconically.

Kate said nothing. There was really nothing to say. Besides, she felt as if a great white light had suddenly broken over her, rendering her temporarily dumb. In a kind of dream she watched Paul jump out to the landing stage, tie up the boat and hold out a hand to her. Still in a dream she followed him to the car. The heat was drying his clothes on him and they were steaming gently as he got in behind the wheel. She was hot and sticky herself, but she was barely aware of it.

The one thing that she was aware of, the one blinding revelation, was that she loved this man beside her, which was quite a different matter from being *in* love with him—from wanting to touch him, to feel his mouth on hers and his hands on her body. This was something that included all that, but was something infinitely deeper.

And infinitely more dangerous.

Back at his apartment, Paul poured them both a long, cool drink and then departed to the shower room. He returned looking fresh and groomed, in a chocolate brown silk robe, his dark hair glistening, and a tang of toilet water about him. He padded across the room in bare feet and sank into the sofa, next to Kate.

'That's better,' he sighed. 'A new man! How do you feel, Kate? Would you like to take a shower? You look delightfully cool, but you're a cool girl, aren't you?' His eyes met her, glinting under their long lashes.

Her heart jolted. He was sitting much too near and she had an overpowering desire to slide her hands down the silk of his gown on to the brown, muscular legs beneath. What an idea! She must be getting utterly shameless. She fixed her eyes steadily on the long, bony feet, sinking into the carpet, and said lightly, 'I'll be okay until I get back to the hotel. Oh, look!' She let out a gasp. 'Your foot—it's bleeding!'

A thin crimson gash ran down the side of his left foot and disappeared under the sole, oozing blood on to the oatmeal-coloured carpet. He regarded it in disgust. 'Blast! I must have caught it on that bloody sampan when I lifted the kid on board.'

Kate said anxiously, 'It looks deep. Shouldn't you go and have it attended to?'

He shook his head. 'No need. I had my jabs only a few weeks ago when I cut my hand on some broken glass, down at my cottage. I must be getting accident-prone.'

'But it should be bandaged. I'll do it for you— have you got a first-aid box?'

'Yes, of course, but I can manage myself.' He got to his feet.

'No,' she said firmly, 'I'll do it. I've got my first-aid certificate.'

He slanted a grin at her as they went into the bathroom. 'Girl Guides?'

'That's right,' she said coolly. A little grey

mouse of a vicar's daughter *would* be a Girl Guide, wouldn't she? '*And* I captained the fourth form hockey team, if you're interested.'

Laugh at that, Mr Sophisticated Caister. I bet none of your girl-friends ever lit a camp fire or wielded a hockey stick in their glamorous lives. 'Now, hold your foot under the cold water until it stops bleeding.'

The first-aid box was in his bedroom. He sat on the side of the bed while she knelt and applied a dressing, then a bandage. Paul sat quite still and didn't say a word while she worked, but she felt his eyes on her all the time and she made herself breathe evenly and slow down her movements while she executed a neat figure-of-eight bandage. His flesh was smooth and firm and her hand lingered on it for a moment when she had finished. 'There, how does that feel? Not too tight?'

She looked up and met his eyes and found she couldn't look away again.

'It feels wonderful,' he said huskily. He leaned over and put his hands under her elbows and lifted her to the bed beside him. 'And you feel wonderful too.'

His arm slipped round her waist and closed over her breast and her senses reeled. She should have pulled away, but she was totally incapable of moving. Her muscles wouldn't work and even her bones seemed to have melted into weakness as she leaned against his firm body, covered only by the silk gown. His other arm went round her, turning her towards him holding her tightly, so that only two flimsy layers of material lay between them.

Paul pulled her down on to the bed beside him

and she saw his face above hers, very close, the dark eyes glittering. She closed her own eyes, waiting for the touch of his mouth on hers.

His mouth came nearer. 'I didn't mean this to happen,' he muttered against her lips before his mouth closed round them. The kiss was deep and probing, as if he would have fused their two mouths into one. His hands moved over her, finding the sensitive places until she gasped with mindless delight. Her hands went round his neck, her fingers twining the thick damp strands of hair convulsively, then pressing themselves against the sinewy nape, while she responded to his kiss with a passion she hadn't known she possessed. Dimly she was aware that all the long, hot hours she had been waiting for this, longing to be in his arms, to feel his kiss.

Then, with a suddenness that sent a shock wave all through her, he pushed her away from him, unlocking her hands from his neck. She opened her eyes, staring blankly, to see that he had got off the bed and was walking across to the window, tightening the belt of his silk robe round him.

Kate pushed herself up on the bed, shivering, one hand against her burning cheek. 'W-what's the matter?' she quavered.

He spun round and his face was dark, the thick brows drawn together. This was the old Paul, the one she thought had disappeared. 'The matter is that I shouldn't have started this bloody silly game at all. I'd never have brought you out here if I'd thought about it a bit longer.' He looked keenly across the room at her. 'You're a virgin, aren't you?'

Her head went up in a gesture of unconscious

pride. 'Yes, I am. Is there anything wrong in that?'

He groaned. 'Everything. Now, get out, for God's sake, and let me get some clothes on.'

Kate stood up stiffly. She felt as if her limbs wouldn't obey her, but somehow she managed to get into the bathroom, where she swilled her face and neck and hands and ran a comb through her dishevelled hair. She took a wet cloth into the sitting room and rubbed at the stain on the carpet. When she had done her best with it she rinsed the cloth out under the cold water tap and hung it over the edge of the basin carefully.

Then, feeling like death, she went back to the sitting room and sat down to wait.

CHAPTER SIX

At last Paul came in. He was dressed for the evening now, very tall and elegant in his dark trousers and white jacket. He went across the room to the cabinet. 'Something to drink before we go?' His tone was casual; Kate might have been a friend who had just dropped in; that scene in the bedroom might never have happened.

'No, thank you,' she said, relieved that at least her voice was steady.

He poured himself a short drink and came and stood looking down at her. 'Now I'll tell you what's going to happen. I'm going to take you back to your hotel, and when you're ready we're going to dine at a restaurant. After that, I shall escort you back, say goodnight, and take my departure in a civilised manner.'

He tossed off his drink and put the glass down. 'You may not believe this, Kate, but I regret what's happened. I accept that it's been my doing and I admit that when I saw you again yesterday my first thought—when I'd got over the transformation that Polly had made in your appearance—was that it would be pleasant to have an affair with you, if I could bring you round to my way of thinking. I'm sorry about that now, in the circumstances I feel I've been less than fair to you.'

He went over and poured himself another drink. She looked at his back, straight and firm in the white jacket. He had combed down his dark hair where her fingers had thrust themselves into it. It was drying now and it curled slightly into his neck.

She swallowed, feeling a kind of numb agony. She had never felt so humiliated in all her life. He must have known—last night and again just now—how willingly she had responded to his lovemaking. If he had slapped her face or thrown her across the room she couldn't have felt more abysmally rejected. Instead, he was standing there telling her in his arrogant way that she didn't really interest him.

She spoke to his back. She said, 'I accept your apology, but it wasn't really necessary. Your—behaviour—didn't bother me. I accepted it as part of the game that you—you blackmailed me into playing.'

He turned and walked back to her, a suspicious glint in his eye. 'You were playing it very convincingly.'

Kate shrugged. 'I didn't have much choice, did I? I shouldn't have been strong enough to fight you off, so I thought I might as well enjoy it. You're an attractive man, as you very well know. You make love very cleverly.'

'Good God, you——' The words died away on his lips, their angry sound echoing through the room. He was really furious, she saw that, and she had a moment of savage satisfaction. She hated him, hated him, she told herself, for what he had done to her.

He was glaring at her, the dark brows drawn together, but she refused to let herself look away or drop her eyes. She regarded him steadily and said, 'Do you still want to go on with the game—or am I not giving satisfaction?'

His hand went up as if he would like to strike her, then he dropped it with sudden weariness, turning away from her. 'Oh yes,' he said. 'I can't——'

For a moment she thought he might be going to offer some explanation, but he merely moved his shoulders impatiently and said, 'Come along, Kate, there's nothing to be gained by chewing over the subject. Let's get going.' He strode across the room and held the door open and she walked out before him, her chin held high. She thought she had managed to convince him that the lovemaking that had passed between them meant no more to her than it did to him. But it was a hollow victory. She wished unhappily that she knew what she had done to make him change his attitude towards her.

But she knew only too well that he wasn't likely to tell her. She told herself that it probably fed his ego to be enigmatic and keep her guessing. He was maddening, arrogant, hateful! She ought to hate him—she *did* hate him. Then she remembered his face after he had fished that tiny Chinese baby out of the harbour, and she stopped trying to convince herself. She knew that this man had the power to hurt her beyond bearing, and she resolved that whatever happened in the days ahead she must never forget that it was all part of a game.

They dined later at one of the restaurants in the hotel where Kate was staying and the meal passed pleasantly enough, although all the time Kate sensed that Paul was on his guard, keeping the conversation impersonal as he told her a little about the Barn Trekker Corporation and their activities. Afterwards they wandered through the hotel's spacious arcade where the shops were still open.

Paul stopped in front of one where ornaments and jewellery were displayed in glittering colour. 'You need something to wear with that dress,' he said. 'Haven't you any costume jewellery? Didn't Polly provide any?'

'Only this.' She lifted her hand where the diamond ring sparkled. 'I understood,' she said distantly, 'that it was intended for someone else.'

He took her hand in his and looked down at the ring sombrely. 'Yes,' he said. 'I wish I could have bought you a different one, but there wasn't time. I'm sorry.'

She shrugged. 'It didn't make any difference to me. I'll take good care of it and let you have it back safe and sound when the time comes.' She removed her hand gently from his clasp.

'Oh, to hell with that,' he said roughly. 'Come on, I'm going to buy you something pretty for you to keep.'

Inside, the shop was brim-full of beauty, with antiques and objets d'art; with handpainted Chinese scrolls, vases and bowls, beads of amber, ivory Buddhas.

'How about this?' Paul picked out a clasp bracelet in gold filigree ending in a dragon's head, with corals for eyes. 'Do you like it?'

He clasped it on her white, slender wrist and stood back to admire the effect, his hand still on her arm. Where his fingers touched her flesh a flame seemed to flare up, eating its way through her body, leaving her weak and shaken. There was a mirror on the wall near where they were standing and she saw the picture they made, in a kind of frozen tableau: there was Paul and herself, close together, he in his slim black trousers and white evening jacket leaning over her possessively (or that was how it looked) she in the coral-pink dress which Polly had said did wonderful things for her complexion, the gold bracelet glinting on her wrist, her pale hair loose around her shoulders and her cheeks nearly as pink as her dress. And the small Chinese shopkeeper nodding and smiling at them both.

Then the picture dissolved, Paul stepped away and the shopkeeper came forward hopefully. 'A wedding ring also?' he suggested. He held a velvet tray in front of Paul's eyes. 'Very beautiful wedding rings.'

'No, I think not.' Paul waved it away and began to settle on the price of the bracelet.

Kate stood in the shop entrance and waited until he joined her. She felt oddly dazed, as if she had seen a vision of some sort. The way they had looked in the mirror—she and Paul together and the little man in black standing before them—it had looked exactly like a wedding.

Paul came up, tucking his wallet away in his pocket, looking like a man who has concluded a satisfactory bargain. She glanced uncertainly at him, touching the bracelet. 'Thank you very much,' she said. 'It's beautiful. But you really needn't have spent so much money—I could have bought myself some bits and pieces, with the generous salary you're paying me.'

He frowned. 'Salary? Oh, your bank account. I don't look on that as salary, more as a gift. The bracelet's a gift, too. Think of it as conscience money if you like. I haven't treated you very well, Kate.'

They strolled together along the wide arcade

and Kate's heart sank. With everything he said, everything he did, he seemed to be putting up a higher and higher barrier between them. If he had actually said, 'Don't build any hopes that those kisses had any serious intention,' he couldn't have made it plainer. With a woman from his own set he wouldn't find it necessary to issue a warning; making love would be quite casual and they would both know it. But she wasn't one of his own set, she was still a little grey mouse of a vicar's daughter. He had fancied her for a brief moment, but he didn't want her to get any ideas into her head.

She pursed her lips and drew a little further away from him. Well, she certainly wouldn't!

They had arrived at the lifts now. 'What would you like to do?' Paul asked. 'Another drink or a coffee before I leave you?'

'No, thanks,' she said. 'I'd like to go straight up to my room, I feel rather tired.'

He didn't try to persuade her; probably he was only too pleased to get away from her, she thought dismally. 'I'm going to be busy tomorrow,' he said. 'What will you do with yourself?'

'I'll find plenty to do,' she assured him lightly. 'I'll love poking round the shops in Central District. I want to write my letters home. And I'd like to look up Mrs Locke—she's the widow of a retired government official. I met her on the plane.'

Paul looked relieved. 'Sounds harmless enough,' he smiled. 'You won't be bored?'

'I can't imagine being bored in Hong Kong,' she said brightly.

He glanced at her. 'You haven't heard any more of Laura Nichols?'

'Not a word.' Kate laughed. 'I expect her in-
vitation was just a polite gesture. I don't suppose
she really wants to trail me round all the tourist
sights.' She watched his face as she spoke. There
was something between him and Laura Nichols,
she was sure, something he didn't want to tell her
about.

He pressed the lift button. 'I hope she'll leave
you alone. This Mrs Locke sounds a much more
suitable companion for you.'

'Suitable!' Kate couldn't repress a giggle. 'You
sound like a Victorian chaperone!'

He didn't smile. 'I'd prefer it if you didn't have
too much to do with Laura,' he said in his most
arrogant tone.

This was far too much like a directive from on
high for Kate to take. She lifted her chin a fraction. 'I'm sorry, Paul, but we're living in the
twentieth century and you really can't give me
orders as to who my friends shall be, even though
you are supposed to be my fiancé.'

The lift arrived and she stepped inside. 'Good
night,' she said with a flashing smile. 'Thank you
for the dinner and my bracelet. You'll ring me
tomorrow evening?'

She pressed the button without waiting for his
reply and just got a faint glimpse of his dark,
frowning face before she was borne out of sight.

It was too much to hope that she would sleep
right away; her mind was in turmoil. She took
her time over undressing, drank a bottle of Coca-
Cola from her 'bar' on top of the fridge, and did
her best to concentrate on one of the books she
had brought with her to read on the plane, before
turning off the light and settling down to sleep.

She would *not* allow herself to brood over the

day that had just passed, to try to fit Paul's behaviour into any sort of pattern that satisfied her.
She would *not* let her hand linger on the dragon
bracelet that was still on her wrist. He had told
her to look upon it as conscience money because
he was sorry about the way he had treated her.
Couldn't she just accept that as the plain truth
and not keep on remembering the way his hand
had held her arm when he put the bracelet on—
as if he were reluctant to let her go? Couldn't she
forget that vivid little reflection in the mirror—
if they were taking their marriage vows?
Couldn't she, she demanded savagely of herself,
grow up and accept the truth?

It was at that point that the memory slid into
her mind. It came clear and complete like a remembered tune. She could hear the words again
just as she heard them spoken in Paul's office:

'And what will you do if the girl really falls for
you, have you thought of that?' Polly had asked,
just as Kate walked into the outer office.

And Paul, in his most arrogant tone, had re-
plied, 'I can deal with that if and when it happens. But naturally I'll take good care to see that
it doesn't.'

Kate squirmed, remembering. But at least she
had her answer now. He *hadn't* taken good care
and it *had* happened, and he knew it. So now he
was dealing with it.

Now she was sure, she felt cold and quite calm.
The bracelet was still on her wrist. She pulled it
off and the dragon's mouth dug into her skin, but
she hardly noticed the pain. In the light that
came in from the street below she found her way
to the dressing table and buried the bracelet deep
in a corner of the top drawer, under a pile of

cotton tops and underwear. There it would stay, she resolved, until she could hand it back to him, together with his ring.

Kate was in her bedroom, just putting the finishing touches to a letter home, when Laura Nichols telephoned the following afternoon. 'Katy? How are you, my dear? Howard and Max have gone off with Mike to see the new factory and I'm all alone and simply screaming with boredom. You really must come and talk to me. You will say yes, won't you?'

'Of course,' said Kate, adopting a social voice without much difficulty. 'How lovely of you to ask me.' If Paul was angry, she thought grimly, that was his business.

'Oh, marvellous! Give me half an hour or so and I'll come and pick you up.'

In the same voice, liberally sprinkled with sugar, Kate said she would look forward to that. Then she replaced the receiver, a small satisfied smile playing round her mouth, and opened the sliding door of the wardrobe to select a dress that would help her to rise to the occasion of meeting Laura Nichols again.

When Laura arrived at the hotel, wearing a deceptively simple black and white dress and driving a racy American sports car in a startling lime green colour, she knew she had chosen right. There was a calculating look in Laura's eyes as Kate stood on the steps of the hotel greeting her: 'So nice of you to ask me!'

'My dear Katy, I'm delighted, and you look absolutely enchanting in that silvery thing—it's so right with your eyes and your lovely fair hair. I love the tiny black check and that wide panel—so clever.' Laura laid a finger on the skirt. 'Pure silk chiffon, isn't it?'

Kate pulled a face. She knew how much the dress had cost. 'I imagine so,' she said drily.

Laura gurgled with laughter. 'You'll think me terribly nosey, but I just love nice clothes. They do such a lot for a girl, don't you think? Now, come along and we'll drive back to my place for coffee and a lovely talk. I've been so looking forward to Paul bringing his girl out here—it's lovely to have a kindred spirit to talk to.'

There was one blessing, Kate decided, as Laura drove noisily and showily up the steep turns of the Peak road, she didn't have to think of anything to say. Laura talked non-stop all the time about nothing in particular.

But when they had arrived at her exquisite white villa, smothered in semi-tropical flowers and shrubs near the top of the Peak, and had settled down on the veranda overlooking the harbour, the talk became very personal indeed.

'Now, my dear, you must tell me *all* about yourself.' Laura lay back in a wicker lounger, a satin cushion behind her head, her slanting green eyes gleaming with curiosity. 'Paul is such a *dear* friend and I'm so longing to know about the girl he's going to marry.'

Kate began to wish she hadn't come. It was one thing to gloat a little because she was asserting herself in defiance of Paul's wishes, it was quite another to sit here and be quizzed by this overpowering woman. She felt uneasily sure that Laura Nichols concealed quite formidable claws beneath her vivacious, rather-too-friendly persona.

A Chinese boy came out to the veranda, pushing a trolley with a tall teapot, decorated in gold

and green, handleless tea bowls to match, and
tiny sandwiches, and while Laura dispensed the
pale, scented liquid, Kate said as much as pol-
iteness required about her family, her childhood
in Devon, their recent move to London.

Laura listened intently, nodding her shining
auburn head above the tea-trolley. 'Yes, as soon
as I saw you I thought—a country girl! There's
something so delightfully wholesome about you,
Katy dear.' She raised her head and the question
came out like a shot: 'And how long have you
known Paul?'

Taken aback for a moment, Kate muttered,
'Oh—quite a short time, really.' She fixed her
gaze on the luxuriously spreading flowers and
foliage beneath the veranda. 'What a beautiful
garden you have.'

Laura pulled a rueful face. 'Oh dear, am I
really being so inquisitive? Yes, I suppose I am.
I'm an interfering, prying wretch, but you must
forgive me, my dear. I liked you from the first
moment I saw you, Katy—though you may have
noticed that I got rather a shock?'

Of course she had noticed, but now she merely
shook her head, feeling vastly uncomfortable.

'Oh yes, you were a real surprise. You see, I'd
been expecting Paul's fiancée to be someone—
well—quite different.'

Kate wished fervently that she had taken Paul's
advice about keeping away from Laura Nichols.
But she wasn't going to allow herself to be intimi-
dated. She smiled smoothly. 'You mean someone
less delightfully wholesome?'

Laura laughed her husky, gurgling laugh. 'You
have a lovely sense of humour, Katy. I can see
why Paul fell in love with you.'

'Thank you,' said Kate, biting into a sandwich.

Laura held her tea bowl between long fingers and sipped delicately and thoughtfully. 'Forgive me for saying this, my dear, but you're so very young and I feel you need another, older woman to guide you through the pitfalls.' She put down her cup and leaned forward, touching Kate's arm tentatively. 'You've only known Paul a very short time—your engagement was one of those whirl-wind affairs. I don't know if you know—if he told you——'

Kate had had enough. She looked the older woman straight in the eye and said, 'You mean, do I know that he had a girl-friend already when he met me? Yes, I do know.'

Laura drew a deep sigh of relief. 'Oh, I'm so glad—that makes everything so much easier. I was afraid it was going to be terribly awkward, but you're such a sensible girl, I can see that.'

'I'm not sure,' said Kate, 'what you're talking about, Mrs Nichols.' She spoke very quietly, but a coldness was creeping over her, a feeling of imminent doom.

'Hasn't Paul mentioned it to you yet, then?—I expect he will.'

'Mentioned what?' Kate could have screamed; it was agony to keep her voice under control.

Laura's green eyes narrowed and she looked somehow—triumphant. 'Why, that Gabrielle is coming out to Hong Kong next week. She and two other girls are being sent out from London by the company to act as hostesses at a promotion reception for Barn Trekker's latest toy—a super new ladies' electronic watch. I expect Paul will have told you all about it. Of course, it isn't his department—he's not on the sales side, is he?—

but he'll no doubt be giving Mike his support. There, now you know, Katy dear, and I'm sure you'll carry it off splendidly when you meet Gabrielle.' She laughed huskily. 'After all, we're civilised people, aren't we? Mike always says——'

Kate wasn't listening. She wasn't thinking either, for her mind felt quite numb. Later, she would have to face this new challenge, but not now. All she longed to do now was to run away— far away from the whole wretched painful situation.

Men's voices sounded in the room behind them and Howard and Max Stenz came out on to the veranda.

Howard dropped into a chair, mopping his damp brow. 'Gee, I thought we had it hot in New York, but this is ridiculous!' He beamed at Kate. 'Good to meet you again, Miss Kate.'

Laura summoned the Chinese servants and drinks were brought for the two men. Max came and sat beside Kate, leaning forward eagerly to talk to her in his pleasant drawl while his father showed every sign of being happily entertained by Laura, who poured his drinks, fluttered her long white hands around him, and flirted quite blatantly, using her husky laugh and her sliding green glance to full effect.

Kate thought of Michael, her nice husband who had, it seemed, had to go back to his office, and felt rather sickened. She stood up, thanked Laura for the tea and said she must be getting back to her hotel.

Max Stenz was on his feet immediately and Laura turned her smile upon him. 'Max, be a darling and see Kate back, will you? I'm sure you can handle my car. Goodbye, Kate my dear, it's been lovely having a chat. We must meet again very soon. I'll ring you.'

Kate found herself back in the lime-green car, with Max beside her. He turned to her with his wide, boyish grin. 'What I figured is we might go by way of the Peak. That way I can take a good look at it and maybe you'd like to as well, Kate. I can't get Pop enthused about seeing places and it's kind of more fun if you have someone with you. Would Paul object, do you think?'

She laughed lightly. 'Heavens, no, Paul wouldn't object. We have Women's Lib in England too, you know.'

'Great!' Max eased the big green car out of the drive and turned its nose up the steep winding hill. He stole a glance at Kate and said, 'Paul's a grand guy.'

Kate laughed again. 'Well, I think so, of course. But you hardly know him, Max.'

He laughed with her, joining in the joke against himself. 'Okay, okay, I was being kinda friendly. But he must be a grand guy, because Mike Nichols says so, and Mike's a grand guy himself.'

Kate slid him a glance. 'That figures,' she drawled teasingly. Max was a nice boy, natural and straightforward. It was a pleasure to be with him.

Max parked the car at the Peak Station and they climbed even further up. The view was breathtaking in the stillness of the afternoon, and up at this height there was even a slight breeze blowing. Far below, the blue of the harbour spread out with all its maritime bustle, and nearer, the rocky prominence was foreshortened so that the tops of the towering white buildings looked like children's toys, set among the lush vegetation. Far away across the harbour the hills rose, layer upon layer, into the misty distance. Max told her that the New Territories were over there. Mike had taken them out there this morning.

'We went right out to the border with China—Communist China,' he told her. His young face looked solemn. 'It's pretty hairy out there—still lots of barbed wire in some places. Hong Kong has a terrific problem with refugees and illegal immigrants. Makes you glad to belong to a free country.'

They were both a little subdued on the walk back to the car. 'I suppose you must get back?' Max asked, rather wistfully.

Kate said she was afraid she must, but she allowed him to persuade her to sit for a while in the garden café and drink a fruity soft drink among the brilliant flowers and the palms that threw dappled shade, while black and white butterflies, larger than any Kate had ever seen, flapped and settled.

'I enjoyed our little expedition, thank you so much.' She smiled up at Max as the green car drew into the forecourt of her hotel a little while later. It was still only late afternoon; there would be plenty of time to shower and change before Paul contacted her after his day's work. She felt that she had managed things reasonably well—especially getting away from Laura Nichols and her hints and innuendoes.

'Me too,' grinned Max. He lifted her left hand where the diamond ring glittered. 'It's a darned shame about this.' The grin widened.

'Isn't it?' she teased, dimpling up at him. 'Goodbye, Max.' She slipped out of the car,

stood for a moment watching while Max eased it
round and headed for the road, lifting a hand in
salute.

She waved back and turned, smiling, towards
the hotel entrance. Then her heart seemed to
bounce up into her throat.

Paul stood there, beside the wide glass door,
and his face was as black as thunder.

There was no time to compose herself. Still
smiling, she walked up to him. 'Hullo, you're off
early, aren't you? I didn't think you'd be away so
soon.'

'So I saw,' he said curtly. 'I suppose that was
Mrs Locke, the widow of the retired Government
official?'

She flicked a glance at the dark, sardonic face
above her own. He might have been fooling, but
he wasn't, and she didn't like the way his mouth
curled into a sneer.

'Don't be ridiculous,' she said crossly, lifting
her chin, and made to walk past him into the
hotel.

His arm barred her way, rigid as steel. 'Oh no,
you don't,' he snapped, his eyes on her flushed
cheeks. 'You're coming back with me. We have
things to talk over.'

Just for a second she thought of defying him,
but the look on his face made her change her
mind quickly. He looked, at this moment, perfectly capable of picking her up bodily and
dumping her in his car.

She shrugged. 'As you like,' she said airily, and
walked before him to the white monster in the car
park.

They drove in complete silence to his apartment and, still in complete silence, went up in the

lift. Kate walked to the window of the sitting room and then turned and faced Paul; by now she reckoned that she had had time to pull herself together sufficiently to keep her cool and hold her own against him if he really wanted a fight.

'Well,' she asked, 'what have I done that's so dreadful?'

He came towards her slowly. 'I think you know.' His tone was dangerously quiet. 'I warned you when you first came out here that there was to be no fooling around when I was working. I know the way gossip can spread in this place, and I don't intend my fiancée to be seen driving around with other men.'

She sank down on to the settee, spreading her arms lightly across the top. 'Really, Paul! You're making it sound like some—some assignment in a Victorian melodrama. If you must have an explanation—and I suppose as your employee I owe you one——' she saw his eyes snap angrily at that '—then this is how it happened. Laura Nichols called for me and took me to her villa for tea. Howard and Max Stenz arrived just as I was leaving and Laura asked Max to drive me back, that's all. Quite innocent!'

'He drove you straight back? No detours on the way?'

She met his gaze blandly. 'Oh yes, I forgot. He took me to the Suzie Wong district, to an intimate little bar, and he booked a private room and——' she rolled her eyes expressively, then her face changed. 'Don't be silly, Paul.'

He was standing before her now, so close that his size blocked out the light from the window. 'What are you trying to do to me?' he breathed very softly.

Her heart was beating like a drum now. She had gone too far and she knew it—you didn't bait a man like Paul Caister. She passed the tip of her tongue over her dry lips. 'Still playing a game,' she said in rather a small voice.

'For one so young you play the game very expertly, Miss Kate Reynolds,' he said, leaning forward to put his arms either side of her against the sofa.

She glanced sideways for escape, but there was none, so she took refuge in bravado. 'You can't live to be nearly twenty-one these days without knowing what the love game is all about,' she said unsteadily, 'even if you don't want to play it yourself.'

He was smiling now, a hard, grim smile that she didn't like at all. 'And I haven't lived to be nearly thirty-three without knowing that a girl often means yes when she says no.'

His face came closer and his mouth locked round hers. She drew in a gasping breath and for a moment her body went rigid. Then she felt herself relax. Her lips softened beneath his, parting to the sensual exploration of her mouth, and shivers of delight passed over her and through her, one after another. He lowered himself to the sofa, forcing her on to her back, his mouth still clinging to hers, one leg thrown across her, holding her so she was unable to move, even if she had had the strength to do so.

She had never known pleasure like this, delirious pleasure that was almost pain. After a moment her hand went to his back, pressing him down against her, feeling the soft yielding of her breasts against the hardness of his chest. It was madness and danger and bliss.

'Paul,' she gasped, 'oh, darling!' as he pulled her dress off her shoulders to allow his hands to go where they wished. With every moment that passed the fever in her blood heightened until she could have denied him nothing that he wanted. She clung to him with rising passion.

Then something changed; his weight had gone from her and he was holding her two arms, almost gently disengaging himself. She opened her eyes and saw that he was smiling, a strange, satisfied smile.

'Okay,' he said. 'That's it, Kate. That's as far as I can trust myself. At least I've learned a thing or two about you. Maybe you've learned a thing or two about yourself.' He got to his feet, buttoning his shirt, and then went over to the cupboard and poured himself a drink.

Kate pulled her dress back over her shoulders with shaking hands as she seethed inside with shame and resentment. He was just a beast, a callous hateful beast! He was exactly the man she had first thought him after all. For a while, yesterday, she had imagined things in him that just weren't there. The way he had dived in after that child had been merely a reflex action from his school training, probably. Inside he was cold all through, cold and calculating. He had deliberately punished her, humiliated her, merely because she had disobeyed him and then had the temerity to laugh at him.

She got to her feet. 'I *have* learned something. I've learned for sure something I guessed about you from the first moment we met.'

'You still find me unlovable?' he mocked.

'I think you're a bastard,' she said between her teeth.

His brows went up. 'Tut-tut, what language for a vicar's daughter! Daddy would be shocked.'

Kate was shocked herself; she had never used the word before in her life. But this man brought out the worst in her.

She got to her feet. Her knees were quivering but her voice was steady. 'I should like to go back to my hotel, please.'

'Certainly. May I offer you some dinner?'

She looked at him, lounging back against the tall cupboard, glass in hand, and remembered that Jerry had first called him a bastard—that was before she had ever seen him. Jerry had been right.

'No, thank you,' she said coldly. 'I'll have something in my room and go to bed early. I have a headache.' That was true, too.

Paul nodded. 'That suits me, I have some work to get through. I'll ring for a taxi to take you back and then I can get down to it straight away.'

'Thank you. I'll go down and wait outside for it.' She had to get away from him, away from those probing dark eyes that seemed to be stripping the clothes from her body and the thoughts from her mind with equal ease.

He shrugged. 'As you please.' He crossed the room and opened the door for her. 'Au revoir, then—*darling* Kate.'

Kate didn't wait for the lift. She stumbled along the passage and down the stairs and his mocking voice followed her as she went.

CHAPTER SEVEN

THE buzz of the telephone beside her bed wakened Kate from a heavy sleep next morning. She stretched out a hand for it, dragging herself back from the oblivion she had sunk into just before dawn, after a restless, miserable night.

'Yes?' she mumbled.

'Good morning, Kate,' came Paul's voice, crisp and businesslike. 'Sleep well?'

She pushed herself up on to one elbow, forcing her mind into clarity, recalling the way they had parted last night. He mustn't have the satisfaction of knowing he had the power to give her sleepless nights.

'Very well, thank you.' That was better; reasonably wide awake and alert.

'Good. Now, listen. I have one or two jobs to do first thing, then I'll be with you later in the morning, so mind you're there when I arrive. I don't want to have to hang around the hotel again, waiting for you. Okay?'

'Okay.' She couldn't resist adding an ironic '——sir!'

'Ha!' Paul's voice came grimly over the line. Then the phone went dead.

She replaced the receiver slowly, pushing the hair out of her eyes, and immediately the heavy, dark misery was with her again. Gabrielle was coming out to Hong Kong next week and—however she looked at it—that pointed inescapably to the fact that she herself would be redundant from then on. The game would be over.

The turmoil of thoughts started up again, she hadn't the power to stop them. Would Paul send her back to England straight away? That would be bad for his image, surely? He wouldn't want to appear to his friends and colleagues the kind of man who would ditch his fiancée for another girl—a girl more obviously beautiful, glamorous, sophisticated—sexy, would he? She shivered in the cool, air-conditioned room and got out of bed to find a wrap, huddling herself into it as she rang room service for coffee.

'No, nothing to eat, thank you, just coffee.' The thought of eating breakfast made her throat choke.

When the boy had brought a tray of coffee she got back into bed, sipping the dark hot liquid gratefully. But the thoughts still revolved round and round in her mind.

Gabriëlle *must* be looking for a reconciliation. It would be too much of a coincidence that she was merely coming out here for the reception. She knew that Paul was in Hong Kong. She was a top model—it wouldn't be hard for her to work it so that she would be sent out with the team.

Did he know she was coming? Had she written—or phoned him? Paul darling, I've been such a fool, can you forgive me and can we start again? Kate's mouth curved cynically. Evidently the Mexican oil tycoon that Polly had mentioned in connection with Gabrielle hadn't come up to scratch.

And what part had Laura Nichols had in all this? Kate hadn't liked the woman, but she had seemed sincere enough, in her gossipy way, about wanting to issue her warning. And what had she to gain, anyway? Kate supposed she ought to be grateful.

Next week—just four days away—and then she would be on a plane going home, and she wouldn't see Paul Caister again.

She should be glad, she told herself savagely. She had always despised the women you hear about who cling on to their love for men like Paul—men who just used women for their own selfish ends. Uncaring, unfeeling, utterly selfish.

She pressed her lips together hard as the tears glazed her eyes. 'But I love him,' she said aloud, almost defiantly, as she crossed to the shower room. 'And I'm just going to stick it out and see what happens.' As she stripped off and stepped under the tepid shower, the ache inside her seemed to be growing and spreading until it engulfed the whole of her from top to toe.

She dressed slowly and carefully in a cream skirt and scarlet-and-cream top, making up her face meticulously as Polly's friend had shown her, brushing her hair to a fine gold sheen and letting it hang loose to her neck, concentrating on every stage to keep her mind from thinking.

When she couldn't stretch it out any longer she started a letter home. She had posted one only yesterday, but it would be just as well to alert them to the fact that she might be home much earlier than they expected her.

She gave them a picture of the Nichols' beautiful villa, of the view from the top of the Peak, not leaving out the darker side of the island—the thousands upon thousands of refugees, crowded together in high-rise tenements and shanty towns. 'I have heard about them but haven't seen them yet—it's not a place to take visitors to—

and anyway, I may be returning a little earlier
than——'

The telephone buzzed. 'Miss Reynolds? Mr
Caister is asking for you, miss, in the lobby,' the
pretty Chinese voice, with its faint American in-
flection, told her.

Paul was sitting at a table under a palm facing
the lifts. He must have been watching for her, for
he rose immediately she appeared. Kate's heart
gave its familiar lurch at the sight of him, handsome and elegant and suave in light putty-
coloured slacks and a shirt of the same shade,
throwing his brown, sunburned skin into dra-
matic contrast.

He was smiling at her with delighted tenderness, something that threw her completely off
balance until she saw the reason for it. He kissed
her lightly, took her hand and led her back to the
table. 'See who I've got here for you, darling,' he
said.

Mrs Locke was sitting there, waiting with
pleased expectancy. 'Well, this *is* nice. How are
you, Kate?'

Kate swallowed. 'Lovely to see you again, Mrs
Locke. I was going to look you up very soon,
wasn't I, Paul?' She darted him a baffled glance.

He smiled broadly. 'Yes, wasn't it lucky that I
found I'd already met Mrs Locke when I was
here before? The fact had escaped me for a
moment when you mentioned it, but as soon as I
saw her again I was delighted.'

Mrs Locke laughed her pleasant laugh. 'And I
was delighted to find out who your fiancé was,
Kate, after the hide-and-seek we played at the
airport. Mr Caister has very kindly invited me to
lunch with the two of you, so I suggest we might

go and have a look round the shops first.' She looked up at Paul. 'Where shall we meet you?'

'I leave it to you, Mrs Locke, you're the resident.' Kate was beginning to be vaguely suspicious. All this charm! She could almost see it working on Mrs Locke, although Kate would have said she was the last person to be impressed by masculine charisma. What was he up to now?

Mrs Locke touched her neat grey hair, smiling back at this handsome man standing beside her deferring to her local expertise. 'Well, it depends upon your choice. We can offer you French, English, Swiss, German, American—and, of course, Chinese. Oh, and Italian, Australian, Scandinavian. What sort of food do you like, Kate?'

'Oh, Chinese, please,' said Kate. 'As I'm only going to be here such a *very* short time I want to get all the atmosphere I can.' She slanted a look at Paul as she said it, but he was consulting his watch.

A time and place was fixed to meet, and then Paul left them with a kiss for Kate and a charming smile for Mrs Locke. He looked, thought Kate, extremely pleased with himself. In his devious way he had evidently managed to bring Mrs Locke into the picture with the purpose of acting as a sort of watchdog. And all without Mrs Locke knowing anything about it! Oh yes, very clever, she thought sourly, very calculating! And another reason to dislike him.

But Mrs Locke wasn't to blame for Paul's despicable behaviour, and Kate thoroughly enjoyed her company. She knew Hong Kong, as she said, 'like the back of her hand', and the morning passed with lightning speed and (which was even better) proved so interesting that Kate hadn't time to brood over Paul. Mrs Locke took her to the Yee Tung Village in the hotel shopping arcade. Here they saw the old Chinese arts and crafts being actually demonstrated at the various stalls. Kate spent an hour selecting presents to take home and finally decided on a string of carved, painted wooden beads for Aunt Ella and a wall-hanging in meticulously embroidered Chinese calligraphy for Father. She hesitated about Jerry—the cause of all that had happened—but eventually chose a tiny lacquered box which she could give him or not, as she felt.

After coffee in the garden restaurant, they took a taxi to Central District and wandered round the big stores and the narrow steep streets, with their market stalls and dark little shops, their crowds and colour and noise that seemed to Kate to be the hallmark of Hong Kong. Mrs Locke had stories to tell about every place they went to. 'I wish you were staying longer,' she said as they made their way to the restaurant where they had arranged to meet Paul, 'I would like to show you some of the Chinese temples. There's a wonderful Buddhist monastery on top of a mountain on the island of Lantao, called the Golden Lotus, and there's the Monastery of Ten Thousand Buddhas in the New Territories. There are all these tiny Buddhas arranged in long rows along shelves. Quite fascinating. The Chinese are great on festivals too, but you've missed the most important one—the Chinese New Year Festival in February. You'll be here for the Moon Festival, though, that's next week. That's rather lovely and it's when the Chinese women who are unmarried ask the moon goddess about their future husbands. A bit like our Hallowe'en.'

'Next week!' exclaimed Kate. 'I'm not sure——'

'Oh, you must stay for that.' Mrs Locke laughed. 'Not that you need to enquire about your future husband. You know all about him, don't you?'

'Of course,' Kate murmured. She knew nothing about him—nothing.

Lunch was a success. They were the only Europeans in the restaurant, except for two Germans at the next table, lunching with a Chinese businessman.

Mrs Locke laughed at Kate's face when she was confronted with the menu, printed entirely in Chinese calligraphy. 'This is a real Chinese restaurant,' she explained, 'not the sort you get in London. It's not easy to find your way around unless you can speak a little of the language.'

She herself spoke Cantonese and the waiters certainly understood her. Paul gracefully handed over the business of ordering. 'Just so long as you allow me to pay the bill,' he laughed.

He laughed a lot over lunch. He and Mrs Locke seemed to get along famously together and Kate had never seen him so relaxed and talkative. They had what was called a Yum Cha lunch, which was a sort of cafeteria, except that waitresses brought round trays of food from which they made their selection. The mysterious contents of some of the bowls were a source of amusement to Paul, who chaffed Mrs Locke about her apparently inexhaustible knowledge of things Chinese, but Kate was quiet and subdued, leaving the talking to the other two, and selecting dishes which she thought she could recognise—eggs, shrimps, peas, ham, with bean shoots and fried rice. She had had no breakfast and found she was hungry and enjoying the food.

But all the time she could hardly keep her eyes off Paul. Today he seemed like a different man as he laughed and swopped anecdotes with Mrs Locke about Hong Kong. He looked heartbreakingly handsome, with his thick dark lashes hiding eyes that narrowed into amusement, and his mouth curved and softened into humour.

The change in him would have been exciting and wonderful if she hadn't known the reason for it. He must have heard that Gabrielle was coming out to Hong Kong next week.

He turned towards her, putting his hand warmly over hers, smiling into her eyes. 'Happy, darling? Everything okay?'

She nodded dumbly, forcing a returning smile, her inside quivering at the touch of his hand. 'Lovely!' she answered, conscious of the look Mrs Locke was bestowing on the two of them—the benign look reserved for young lovers. If she only knew, Kate thought bleakly.

Paul glanced at his watch and put down his bowl of tea. 'Goodness, I must go, I've got a conference awaiting me. I'll pick Kate up at your apartment, Mrs Locke, when I've finished.' He paid the bill, as the waitress counted the number of empty and half-empty bowls and baskets on the table, and took his leave, courteously bowing to Mrs Locke and pressing Kate's hand.

What a performance! she thought peevishly. Anyone would have thought he'd won the Irish Sweep.

Mrs Locke sighed, her eyes soft. 'What a lucky girl you are, Kate, to have a man like that. He's absolutely charming!' Fortunately she was reaching for her handbag and didn't see Kate's expression.

'I hope,' she went on, 'that you won't be too bored with the company of an elderly lady. Mr Caister seemed a little worried that you should be on your own while he was working, so he suggested that I should show you round as he couldn't be with you himself. Tomorrow I'm visiting some Chinese friends and they would be delighted if you would accompany me. It would be interesting for you to see the inside of a real Chinese house, I'm sure.'

There was no way Kate could refuse—and anyway, she didn't want to. She liked Mrs Locke and found that her sensible good humour and fund of amusing stories and local knowledge made a stout defence against her own inclination to sink into unhappy fear about what the next few days would bring. But all the same she was resentful that Paul should so obviously consider she needed a watchdog. That bit about being afraid she would be bored simply didn't hold water.

They dined together at her hotel that evening and she tackled him about it. 'You didn't tell me you already knew Mrs Locke,' she said, keeping her eyes on her plate.'

'I didn't,' he said blandly, 'but it wasn't too difficult to get to know her. The widow of a retired Government official—very easy to trace. I deal with more difficult jobs than that every day.'

She looked up at his face, bland and confident. 'Why did you bother?'

His brows lifted maddeningly. 'Don't you know? I thought she would keep you out of mischief for the rest of the time you're here.'

'And that won't be very long, of course, will

it?' She made it sound like an innocent question.

Paul shot her a narrowed glance. 'What do you mean?'

She shrugged. 'Well, your work here will be coming to an end fairly soon, you said, and then my services will no longer be required.'

'I suppose that's one way of putting it.' Kate thought she saw a faint smile lurking at the corners of his mouth. 'As a matter of fact it may be sooner than I thought. All the teething problems of the new factory seem to be getting ironed out now, so they won't be requiring my services for much longer.'

'How much longer?' she pressed. She had a great need to know how much longer she had with him before he said goodbye and walked out of her life.

'Certainly not before next week. Mike's got some scheme on for next week—he's arranging a reception at the Hilton for launching one of our new gadgets. It's not really my line of country, but he's asked me to be sure to be here for it. He's chosen the day of the Moon Festival and they're sending some dolly-girl models out from U.K. to grace the occasion. The theory is that lovelies can sell anything,' he grinned.

So he *didn't* know that Gabrielle was coming! He would never have spoken like that of a girl he'd been in love with only a couple of weeks ago. He was due for a shock when he saw her, then, and no doubt a very pleasant shock. One that would change his life.

'So,' he was saying, 'I'm sorry I can't tell you exactly how much longer you'll be here. Mrs Locke says she'll be very glad to entertain you while I'm busy in the daytime. You like her, don't you?'

She gave it up after that, and didn't try any further questions. She told herself that this, after all, was what she had agreed to do, what she had come to Hong Kong for: to act as Paul's fiancée, to play the game his way.

But he hadn't played fair, even if she had. He had made her fall in love with him, and very soon he was going to send her away. She was sure of it, and the certainty was like a heavy stone inside her.

After that the days assumed a pattern. Kate spent the mornings and afternoons with Mrs Locke. One day they visited her Chinese friends at their beautiful new home in Shatin, where the husband had just opened a factory manufacturing plastic articles. Another day they visited the Tiger Balm Gardens, a flamboyantly constructed wonderland, full of grottoes and pavilions with weird effigies from Chinese mythology. They saw the performing dolphins at the Ocean Park and exotic birds at the Botanic Gardens. They went on a harbour cruise in a motorised junk.

When Kate attempted to pay for some of these expeditions Mrs Locke smiled and said merely that Paul was footing the bill. 'He's so sorry that he hasn't the time to show you round himself,' she said, 'and has asked me to be your courier. What a thoughtful young man he is!'

Paul had indeed made a conquest, Kate thought wryly.

But she couldn't help enjoying it all. It was the holiday of a lifetime, in this fascinating, exotic, colourful, overcrowded island. The evenings, when she dined with Paul, had a bitter-sweet flavour. His new personality was still in evidence.

He wwas once again the delightful companion he had been on that trip to Cheung Chau, but there was no man–woman challenge and definitely no lovemaking. He hardly touched her, except for a light kiss on her cheek or forehead when they met.

He must have known that she had fallen in love with him, and he wanted to save himself embarrassment, she concluded dismally, and she tried hard to convince herself that it was better that way, while every nerve in her body quivered when he came near her, and wherever she was she looked for the sight of his dark head above the crowd. It was madness and agony, and the sooner she got away the better. But she dreaded the moment when the blow would fall.

On Wednesday morning Laura Nichols telephoned. 'Katy dear, I've managed to catch you in at last! How are you? I've so wanted to fix up some outings for you, but you were always out when I phoned.'

Trying not to sound too relieved, Kate expressed regret, saying she had friends in Hong Kong and had been spending most of her time with them.

'Oh well, just so long as you've been enjoying yourself that's fine. But we shall see you this evening, shan't we, at the Hilton reception? It's rather clever to fix it on the day of this Moon Festival, don't you think? Adds a little glamour to the occasion!'

Kate murmured something appropriate, then there seemed to be a lull in the conversation and she wondered if Laura had rung off or if the line had been cut. But no! The husky, rather affected voice went on, 'Just to put you on your guard, my dear—the model girls arrive this afternoon and will definitely be appearing. They should have flown in yesterday, but there was a hitch. And Katy, Gabrielle *is* one of them, that's for sure, so——' a gurgle of laughter to show that Laura didn't really mean to be taken too seriously '——be on your guard, my child!'

'Oh, I will,' Kate said brightly, feeling rather sick.

'See you then. Young Max is longing to see you again—you made a real conquest there, Katy.' Another conspiratorial laugh. 'Just as well to have a second male dangling on the end of your hook! 'Bye for now, Katy. Be good.'

'Goodbye.' Kate replaced the receiver, filled with dislike for Laura Nichols. How a nice man like Mike could have married a woman like that was a mystery.

Almost immediately Paul's morning call came through. He telephoned each morning to check on her plans for the day. 'Nothing special,' she told him. 'Mrs Locke has some market shopping to do and then we thought we'd have a lazy afternoon.'

'That fits well.' He sounded satisfied. 'It's this do at the Hilton this evening and I've got to look in. I thought we might dine there first. I shan't be very early getting away, I've got rather a lot to get through today. I'll call for you around seven, okay? Put a pretty dress on to charm our potential customers. Just so long as I'm there to keep an eye on you I'll allow you that in the interest of the firm.'

'Thanks very much.' Kate made herself laugh, but the smile withered and died as she replaced the receiver. It would be Gabrielle that Paul would be keeping an eye on tonight.

But in her room that evening she dressed with care. She wouldn't be able to compete with a willowy, raven-haired beauty with huge violet eyes, but she would have been a fool if she hadn't known she was a pretty girl. And she had gorgeous legs, she knew that too. Maybe Gabrielle's legs were even more gorgeous, but she wouldn't brood about that. At least she was wearing Paul's ring, and that gave her courage.

She would wear the only evening dress that he hadn't seen yet—she had been keeping it for some special occasion, and this was going to be it. The dress was of ivory ciré satin, with a sleek suppleness that rippled with every movement. The low cross-over top moulded her firm young breasts and the daring slit skirt disclosed her sleek, silken legs, ending in gold-strapped, slim-heeled sandals.

She hardly recognised herself when she looked in the mirror. A very long way away from London on a wet September morning, and a girl in a damp grey mac and rats'-taily hair! Her hair was swept up on top now, smooth and pale and elegant—the right style for the classic elegance of the dress.

Paul was waiting in the foyer for her as she stepped from the lift, her nerves as taut as guitar strings, a smile fixed firmly on her lips.

He took both her hands and held her away, looking her over. 'Very elegant tonight! Not a mouse's whisker in sight. A beautiful white snake instead.'

'Snake? That's not very complimentary. I resent that!'

He pulled her hand through his arm as they

turned to the door, and her knees felt weak at his touch. She leaned against him momentarily, hoping he wouldn't notice. 'My dear child, you haven't studied your Chinese astrology,' he teased. 'To call a woman a snake in the East is the ultimate in compliments.'

Kate glanced up at him and her heart shook. He looked wonderful this evening; he had exchanged the usual white evening jacket for a two-piece suit in some light material the colour of rich black coffee, and a pleated white shirt. No man had any excuse to be so devastating, she told herself. 'And what is the ultimate compliment for a man?'

'I wouldn't know. To call him a tiger, perhaps. Or a dragon.' They were out in the dimness of the car park now and his teeth flashed whitely against the brown of his face. 'I think I fancy the dragon. Breathing fire is more satisfying, surely, than lurking in the bushes.'

That set the key for their conversation over dinner at the Hilton; trivial, frivolous, never a serious word. Since it was the Hilton, the food was no doubt superb, although Kate wouldn't have noticed the difference if they had been served sausage and mash. Everything tasted like sawdust in her mouth and she felt guilty when she thought what it must be costing.

It was a very leisurely meal; Paul seemed in no hurry to join the Barn Trekker reception. But finally he sighed and said, 'Well, I suppose we'd better put in an appearance or Mike will have my blood. I'll find out where the show is.'

They went up to the next floor and along innumerable passages and finally found the suite where the reception was taking place.

They went into an ante-room, where the bar was doing steady business, and which led through into a much larger room. Both rooms were crowded and as they eased their way in Paul muttered in Kate's ear, 'Mostly gatecrashers, I shouldn't wonder, here for the free drinks.'

But he soon found some colleagues that he knew, from the company, and Kate was introduced to a confusing number of men and their wives, whose names she couldn't possibly remember, and a glass was put into her hand, and she smiled and exchanged social chit-chat, while all the time her eyes were probing the moving mass of well-dressed men and women, looking for one girl more beautiful and glamorous than the others, a willowy, raven-haired beauty who must be called Gabrielle.

Mike Nichols came up and talked to her in his pleasant, sincere way, genuinely pleased to see her again. Later she encountered Laura, gaudy in a scarlet trouser-suit. '*So* glad you could come, Katy. *What* a success for Mike! We're simply delighted.' She waved an arm round the crowded room, heavy with the scent of massed flowers and the aroma of cigar smoke. There was no mention of Gabrielle, but Laura looked like a cat that has found a saucer of cream, and Kate didn't doubt that Gabrielle was the reason.

She had got separated from Paul now and found herself in the larger room through the archway, with Howard Stenz by her side, puffing at a huge cigar. 'Barn Trekker sure know how to put on a show,' he beamed at her. 'Seen the new toy of theirs?' He led her across the room to show her the reason for the reception—the tiniest, most delicate ladies' watch she had ever seen in her life, a little gem of a thing. There were several of them, laid out on satin on a table, like presents at a wedding. Some were mounted in stainless steel, some in silver, some in gold. There were fabulous-looking models set with diamonds, others with sapphires and pearls. 'They're very beautiful,' she commented absently, looking round for Paul. Without him beside her she felt lost and vulnerable.

Then she saw him across the room. She turned to Howard Stenz with an apologetic smile. 'Excuse ——' she began, then stopped abruptly.

A very tall girl was weaving her way between the guests. She was certainly making for Paul, but he hadn't seen her yet. She was willowy and raven-haired and she moved with all the grace of a trained model. From this distance Kate couldn't see the colour of the huge, wonderful eyes, but she could guess at the light that shone in them to match the delighted curve of the exquisite mouth. Her dress of deep violet chiffon foamed round her lovely legs as she went, and even across the room, even above the hubbub of chatter and laughter, Kate heard the delighted ring in her high voice as she cried, 'Paul—Paul darling!'

He was half turned away and Kate couldn't see his face; she was to be spared that. But she saw the way he took the hand that Gabrielle stretched out to him, saw the way she reached up and kissed him, putting her arms round his neck— slender white arms weaving round him, holding him fast.

'Miss Kate, are you okay?' Howard Stenz's robust voice reached her from a great distance. She glanced at him vaguely and then her eyes went back to the two across the room. They were talking now, their heads close together, Paul's dark head lowered only a little to be able to reach the dark head of the girl beside him. Kate could see his face now, a little blurred through the smoky atmosphere. She thought he looked very serious, but of course this would be a serious moment for him. What was she saying? 'Paul darling, I've been such a fool—such a *bloody* fool.' (Girls like Gabrielle would use words like that all the time.) 'Are you going to forgive me?'

Of course he would forgive her. Perhaps not too easily, because Paul Caister was a proud man, but quite soon. Even now his arm was round her shoulder, guiding her towards the far door. She was looking up into his face, laughing. Then they had disappeared.

It had all happened just as Kate had rehearsed it in her mind and she should have been prepared. The sick misery that engulfed her was shocking, and for a moment the whole room lurched before her eyes, then straightened itself again. She heard Howard Stenz say, 'Max, this girl's needing to get out of the crush. I guess you might take her outside for a while.'

Max was holding her arm then, taking her down in the lift and out into the courtyard of the great giant of a hotel. 'Pop was right, you're not looking good.' He leaned over her as she sat perched on a low wall.

Kate drew in a deep breath of cool air and felt better. She looked up at Max, large and comforting, towering above her, his bright blue eyes worried.

'Are you okay? Would you like me to go and get Paul?'

'No—no, really,' she said quickly. 'I'm quite all right now. It was just rather hot and crowded in there. I'll stay out here for a while and look at the celebrations. It's the Moon Festival, isn't it?' She had a sudden longing to get away from the hotel and that upstairs room where Paul and Gabrielle were— doing what? She didn't want to think about it.

'Let's walk along and see what's going on, shall we?' She smiled up at Max Stenz, so nice, so ordinary, so anxious to please her, and felt a little comforted.

'Sure, if that's what you'd like.' He took her arm and they wandered out into Queen's Road, past the great towering bank buildings, into the shopping area, where the ladder streets rose steeply from the main road. Here all was celebration indeed and the dense crowds of people seemed almost solid. Tables were set out and laden with fruit and flowers, with bowls of rice and tea, and cakes and incense in painted boxes. There was a sudden explosion of fire-crackers and Kate grabbed Max's arm tightly. Her nerves felt raw and on edge, and the crowds, surging and moving like a solid mass, were a little frightening.

Max insisted on buying her a moon-cake in a decorated tin, then they made their way into a less densely packed area where musicians were playing ancient-looking pipes and stringed instruments.

Max grinned down at her. 'Gosh, that was kind of hairy—like to go back to the peace and quiet of the reception?'

'No!' she said sharply. And then, more calmly, 'What I'd really like, Max, is to get back to my hotel and have an early night. But I don't want to bother Paul—he's helping Mike with the entertaining in there. Do you think you could be an angel and see me back?'

'Sure, if that's what you want.' The young man didn't hide his pleasure. 'I'll borrow Mike's car—I know where he parked it—and run you back.'

At the hotel Max was reluctant to leave. Kate didn't much relish the idea of being alone. 'You've been so kind,' she said. 'Let me buy you a drink before you leave.' Finally, it was an hour before Max managed to tear himself away, promising to explain to Paul when he got back. She thought he looked a little apprehensive as he promised.

'I hope he won't think I've been getting too friendly,' he grinned.

Kate smiled back at him gaily. 'Oh, don't take any nonsense from Paul. I don't.' It would be wonderful to think that Paul might be jealous—wonderful but quite impossible to believe.

After Max left her there was nothing left to do but go to her room. She tried to read, but the print kept blurring before her eyes, and when she looked down out of her window the lights below blurred too. She tried not to let herself think about Paul and Gabrielle together, but she kept seeing again the way those white arms wound round his neck, kept hearing again the clear, high delighted voice crying, 'Paul—Paul darling!' She felt very alone and rather frightened.

Presently the phone buzzed and it must be Paul. Her heart started to race. 'Kate? What's going on? Young Max Stenz has just told me you wanted to leave. I've been looking all over for you. Are you all right?' He sounded more angry than worried about her wellbeing.

'Yes, I'm fine, thanks. I just felt hot and tired and thought I'd like to get away from the crush.'

'But why the hell couldn't you have told me?' Yes, he *was* angry.

'I didn't want to bother you. You were busy with your business friends.'

There was a long silence and she wondered if he had hung up. But then, in an odd, distant voice, he said, 'I see.'

There was another long pause until she could bear it no longer. 'Paul—are you still there?'

'Yes,' he said. 'I was thinking. Look, Kate, stay around tomorrow morning, will you, until I contact you? I'll be with you by eleven at the latest. Now, are you sure you're okay—not ill, or anything?'

It was nice of him to pretend to be worried about her, even at this late point in the conversation. 'I'm fine,' she said. 'I'm just going to bed—I felt like an early night. I'll see you in the morning, Paul.'

'Right,' he said. 'And—Kate——'

'Yes?'

'Look after yourself,' he said, and then there was silence.

She replaced the receiver gently. She could almost feel sorry for him; by now she felt she knew him well enough to be sure that he would have a few guilty feelings about having involved her in all this—all quite unnecessarily, as it happened. But he wasn't to know that Gabrielle meant to come back into his life. He would be irritated too; no man likes to have two women making demands on him.

Slowly she undressed and got into bed. No demands would come from her. It had all been a game and the end hadn't ever been in doubt. She was the loser. Now all that remained for her to do was to leave the playing field as soon as possible.

She hoped with all her heart that it would be very soon indeed.

CHAPTER EIGHT

KATE had just finished dressing next morning when there was a knock on the door. The room boy for her breakfast tray, of course. She went across and unlocked the door, smiling. The room boys at the hotel were cheerful souls and she always had a smile for them.

Paul stood there and the grim look on his face made the smile die on her mouth. 'You're—you're early,' she stammered.

He came in and closed the door and stood with his back to it. 'Sorry to barge in like this. I hadn't time to wait until they called you down.' He looked like a man with only minutes to spare.

Her knees felt suddenly like elastic and she sank down into a chair by the window and waited.

He said, 'I'm not going to say any more about the way you walked out on me last night with Max Stenz. We'll let that ride.'

Kate stiffened, her eyes sparking. How dare he, when he and that girl Gabrielle—— 'I didn't——' she began but he held up a peremptory hand.

'Let me finish, please. The fact is that the whole situation here has got altogether too complicated.'

'Yes,' said Kate. She could agree with that. She looked away from him, out of the window. She was sure what was coming next and she wouldn't let him see her face when the blow fell.

'When you can't untie a knot you cut it,' said Paul. 'So—I'm sorry to shorten your stay here, Kate, but I've decided to send you home straight away.'

She felt herself flinch as if her flesh could feel his words. But only for a moment. She drew in a tight breath and turned to face him.

'When?'

'I've just been on to the travel agents,' he said, 'and there's been a cancellation for this evening's flight. Can you be ready?'

Now it had come she felt very calm. It was like a deep cut; you didn't begin to feel the pain until afterwards. 'Yes, of course,' she said. 'What are the arrangements?'

Paul's face expressed nothing but polite regret. 'I've got a very heavy day ahead and I may not be able to get away in time to see you off. If I can't make it, Josh will come here to collect you, about half past five. That will leave plenty of time. He'll have your ticket, and cash for the journey in U.K. notes. I'll arrange for the balance of the bank account here to be transferred to you in London. Have I got your home address? I don't think I have.' He took out a notebook and scribbled it down.

Kate pulled off the diamond ring and held it out to him, but he shook his head and said, 'Please wear it until you've left Hong Kong. We don't want questions asked. I'll have it back some time,' he added carelessly.

She pushed the ring back on to her finger. 'I'll leave it with your sister when I get home,' she said. She would leave the dragon bracelet too and then that would be the end. Nothing would remain to remind her of Paul Caister—nothing except her memories, and somehow she would have to blot them out. Somehow.

'Well, I think that's all, then,' he said. 'I'm sorry it's ended so abruptly.'

She stood up. Her knees were trembly, but at least she could be sure that his final sight of her wasn't as a crushed heap in a basket chair.

'I'll be glad to go,' she said.

Paul shot her a keen glance under those incredible lashes. 'Is that the truth, Kate?'

'Oh yes. It's been very—interesting—but as you know I wasn't altogether easy about leaving my father.'

He nodded. 'Of course.' They might have been strangers.

There was a short silence, then Kate said, 'This is goodbye, then, Paul.' She didn't know whether her hands moved towards him of their own accord, but if they did he didn't touch them.

He just stood there, looking down at her, his eyes inscrutable and very dark. 'Au revoir,' he said. 'I'll see you again.'

'Goodbye,' she said again firmly. Once in a lifetime for this kind of emptiness was enough.

Paul stood for a moment longer as if he were going to say something else, then he turned and walked out of the room.

Kate stood stiffly where she was until she was sure he had left the hotel, and only then did she crumple on to the bed and let herself begin to cry.

It was Josh who called for her at half-past five, of course. She had known it would be.

'Sorry it's me, Kate. From your point of view, not mine.' The cheery, freckled face under the thatch of red hair looked rueful. 'Paul's been in the thick of it all day and they haven't come out of conference yet. But I'm sure he'll be along before zero hour if he can possibly make it.'

Zero hour, Kate thought, he didn't know how appropriate that was. Zero—nothing—the lowest point—that was exactly how she felt. She had kept going by a sheer effort of will all day, her body empty and numb. She would have been thankful to stay in her room and bury her head in the bedclothes until the time came to leave, but that would have been infantile. Instead she had taken a taxi to Mrs Locke's home, told her the news, and stayed for lunch.

Mrs Locke was sincerely disappointed that she was leaving Hong Kong and Kate felt quite miserable about having to spin a weak story about being worried about things at home. It would have been a relief to confide the whole story to this pleasant, intelligent woman, of whom she had grown very fond in the days they had spent together. But there was no advice she needed, no action she could take, and pouring out her troubles would have merely been self-indulgence, so she went on smiling and talking small-talk until the time came to leave.

Packing didn't take long and she was waiting in the hotel lobby when Josh arrived. At the airport there was more than an hour to wait for her flight to be called, and the minutes ticked away with awful slowness, each one like an hour. A snack meal filled up some of the time. After that they wandered round the bright, modern shopping arcade with its array of watches and cameras and radios. When they had seen all there was to be seen there they sat in the departures lounge and waited.

Conversation had worn thin and Kate could see Josh's eyes searching round rather desperately for Paul to arrive. But Paul wouldn't arrive, she could have told him that, and when, finally, her flight was called she was almost amused at the relief that spread over Josh's pleasant young face.

He checked for the tenth time that she had everything she needed, instructed her about procedure at Heathrow, and finally shook hands enthusiastically.

'It's been wonderful knowing you, Kate, and it's a bind that you can't stay longer, but perhaps we'll meet again when I've finished my stint out here and I'm back in London. I'll be sorry to lose Paul, too, when he leaves, it's been a pleasure to work for him and I've learnt a lot.'

She smiled and thanked him and said all the right things. Only another few seconds now and then all the play-acting and lies would be behind her.

'Goodbye, Josh, and thank you for looking after me.' A gesture of farewell and she was through the barrier, walking blindly towards the plane that would carry her away from Hong Kong and Paul Caister. It hadn't taken her long to fall in love with him; it was going to take a very long time to forget him.

Until she was shown to her seat on the plane she hadn't realised that she would be travelling in first-class luxury this time. Everything was larger and more spacious, but she was in no mood, yet, to appreciate it. It was good, though, not to be packed in closely, good to find herself in a seat next to the window.

It was almost dark outside now, nothing much to be seen except the view across the runways, the other planes shadowy and huge under the lights. She stared out, blinking the tears away. She was glad, *glad*, she told herself fiercely, that Paul hadn't come to see her off. It would have been just more play-acting, prolonging the end of the game. But as the scene outside blurred before her eyes she knew that she had hoped up to the last minute for a miracle, longed with every bit of her to see him just once again.

A stout man in a business suit took the seat next to hers. He nodded, 'Good evening,' and proceeded to take a sheaf of papers out of his brief case. Kate murmured a reply and turned her head away.

At last announcements came over the PA system, seat-belts were fastened, they were moving, taxing slowly, stopping, turning, moving again, then gathered speed and swooshing along the wide rectangular concrete arm that stretched out into the harbour. She could see the dark waters below and knew they were airborne.

She let out a deep sigh as the plane gained height. This was it, then, the end of the game. Below, the kaleidoscope of colour along the waterfront flickered and winked, reflecting red and blue and yellow and green in the water, while points of white light from the villas and apartment blocks on the Peak gleamed like diamonds among the dense darkness of the foliage. It was as if Hong Kong was putting on a special light-show as a gesture of farewell.

Kate sat with her eyes closed as the plane gained height and the lights below were left behind. She opened them again as the stewardess went through her routine of instructions and information about safety. A uniformed man who looked like a head steward came and spoke in a low voice to the stout businessman in the next seat. There seemed to be a little difference of opinion, but finally the stout man put his papers together and moved himself, grumbling, to a seat on the other side of the aisle, further forward.

The steward smiled at Kate. 'Slight mix-up in the reservations, miss,' he told her. 'It does happen now and again.'

A smiling air hostess came round for orders for drinks, suggesting champagne, but Kate shook her head. Champagne was for celebrations and there wasn't anything to celebrate.

'I'll have——' She lifted her head from the wine list and the words froze on her lips. Over the girl's shoulder she saw a man emerge from the front partition and walk slowly down the aisle towards her.

She was dreaming, of course. It had all been too much for her and she was seeing a vision. She put a hand over her heart as if she could stop its wild thumping.

Paul slipped into the vacant seat beside her. 'Hullo, Kate,' he said. 'I only just made it.'

She passed her tongue over her dry lips. 'Paul?' she croaked.

He smiled at her, his dark, long-lashed smile, and the plane and everything in it seemed to be spinning in a rainbow mist. He leaned towards her and covered her hand with his, warmly, strongly.

'Hullo, Kate,' he said again, and—softly, more closely, 'Hullo, darling Kate.'

She struggled for some sort of sanity. 'The— the game's over, have you forgotten?'

He shook his head. 'This isn't a game. This, as

our American friends would say, is for real, my love.' His head came closer, his hair brushed her cheek. 'You *are* my love, Kate, aren't you?'

The feel of his springy hair against her cheek, the smell of his skin, mingled with the astringent tang of the after-shave he used, sent her senses swimming. But she must have time. It was too quick, too utterly stupefying, to believe all at once.

She swallowed. 'How can you be so sure?'

Paul moved away slightly. 'I'm not sure, I've never been sure. But I'm prepared to start changing your mind if you say No. It might be quite amusing for our fellow-passengers.'

His arms came out purposefully, he turned in his seat. 'No, Paul, please!' Kate whispered urgently, her face crimson.

'Go on, then, say it,' he demanded.

'Blackmail! That's what it is,' she wailed, and he drawled,

'I seem to have heard that before from you, Miss Reynolds.'

Their eyes met and held in a long look that seemed to say everything. She had seen his eyes hard, ironic, scornful, angry. She had never thought they could look like this—deep with tenderness. Her inside twisted with an answering tenderness and an urgent need.

'I love you,' she whispered, and tears gathered in her eyes and trickled down her cheeks.

She sniffed and dashed them away hastily as the stewardess arrived. 'Your champagne, sir.'

Paul lifted his glass with its sparkling bubbles. 'To us!'

'To us,' Kate echoed, and then, 'You ordered champagne—you must have been sure of me.'

'I told myself I was,' he admitted,' because if I

couldn't have you it seemed that life would be a howling wilderness.' He chuckled suddenly. 'And I must admit that when you called me a bastard I was somewhat encouraged. Remember?' His eyes probed hers meaningfully and it was as if she were in his arms again.

She smiled softly at him over the rim of her glass. 'You were,' she said. 'You are.'

'Yes,' he said complacently.

There was a long contented silence and then she said, 'Why couldn't you have told me before? When did you know?'

Paul looked thoughtful. 'I think you must have begun to work your magic on me right from that first day—only I was too damned angry to recognise the fact.'

She grinned. 'You were blazing, weren't you?'

'I was,' he said grimly. 'My self-image was badly dented. It's my job to be able to decide whether I'm hearing the truth or hearing lies. That blasted girl!'

Kate touched his hand gently. 'I don't want to hear about it if you'd rather not tell me.' No man takes kindly to being turned down by a girl, Polly had said, and Paul least of all.

He leaned his head back. 'You may as well know,' he said. 'I'd persuaded myself I'd like to marry Gabrielle. I'd taken her out to dinner and I had the ring in my pocket. And then her husband turned up, very, very drunk and hell-bent on making a scene. She'd forgotten to mention that she was married,' he added, with a twist of his lips. 'I imagine she thought if she could really annex me she could get round me to wait until she'd arranged a divorce. I'd made it perfectly plain that I wanted marriage, not an affair, you

see, that's how much of an idiot I was. I've never
been so angry with myself in my life for not
seeing through the girl. But she was very prettily
packaged,' he added cynically.

Kate made no comment. She could almost feel
sorry for Gabrielle now. She was more than
prettily packaged, she was very, very beautiful.

'I knew I'd had a lucky escape,' Paul went on.
'I was out of that restaurant in two minutes flat.
But what made me even angrier was that now I
didn't have a fiancée to bring out to Hong Kong
to defend me from Laura Nichols, who was
making a damned nuisance of herself.'

Kate's mouth quirked. 'Poor darling,' she said
softly. 'You shouldn't be so devastatingly attractive.'

He gave her a look that made the blood beat in
her throat. 'I wondered about you and Laura,'
she said hastily. 'The way she spoke to you—
those intimate little glances. I thought perhaps——'

'No!' Paul exploded violently, and the stout
businessman in front looked round, frowning.
'No,' he repeated more calmly. 'I didn't fancy the
woman in any case, but if I had I should still
have refused with thanks. Mike Nichols is a good
chap and my friend. What he's done to deserve a
wife like Laura I'll never know. He adores her
and hasn't a clue what she's really like. A brilliant
organiser and a blind idiot where his wife is concerned.' He looked sombre for a moment.

'So that,' said Kate quietly, 'is why you
brought me into the game?'

'I was desperate. I'd let them all know in H.K.
that I was bringing my future wife out. Then,
when it turned out that I didn't have a future

wife, I had to make up my mind quickly what to do. That was when you walked into my life like a——'

'—like a little grey mouse walking into a mouse-trap,' Kate giggled, warm with champagne and love.

'—a pretty white snake,' Paul corrected, laying a hand on the lapel of her cream linen safari suit. 'Oh God,' he groaned. 'Would you be terribly embarrassed if I kissed you?'

He was discreet about it, but it left Kate trembling and Paul seemed to have some difficulty in going on with his story.

Eventually he said, 'To continue—I was too optimistic when I thought I'd got out of Laura's clutches. Who was it said hell has no fury like a woman scorned?'

Kate nodded. 'She told me that your—that Gabrielle was coming out to Hong Kong, and warned me that I'd better keep an eye on you.'

'Did she?' he growled. 'Yes, she was hell-bent on making trouble in any way that turned up. I got it all out of her last night. I tackled her and she more or less admitted it. It seems she has a pal in London who runs a model agency and between them they worked it to offer Gabrielle this job. It suited our Gabrielle down to the ground because she was anxious to have another chance to be Mrs Paul Caister. What a hope!'

'Polly thought *she'd* turned *you* down,' said Kate, and added dreamily, 'I was quite sorry for you. I—sort of—made allowances because I thought you were missing Gabrielle.'

'Generous of you,' he said with heavy irony. 'The stark truth was that I couldn't seem to manage to keep my hands off you. I tried to wait—I knew I'd got off on the wrong foot with you.'

'So you didn't know that Gabrielle would turn up last night?' Kate asked rather timidly, and the look he gave her almost reminded her of the times she had seen him blaze with anger. But it passed immediately.

'What do you take me for, my darling? If I'd known I would have told you the whole story and chanced my luck. No, I got the worst shock of my life when I saw her making for me across the room. Apparently her divorce is going through and she didn't see why we couldn't, etc., etc. God! it made me sick. Then, when I'd got rid of her, Laura Nichols told me sweetly that she'd seen you go off with Max Stenz. I was out combing the streets in the middle of that bloody festival, looking for you. It was an hour and a half later when he finally came back.'

He ran a hand distractedly through his hair, living again the frustrations of the night before. 'That was when I decided I was going to get you away, out of it all, as soon as I could. I managed to get the two cancellations, but I wasn't sure until the very last minute whether I could finally wind up my assignment here and join you. I only made it by the skin of my teeth and then I had to practically go on my knees to the head steward to work it so that I got this seat next to you. Fortunately the captain of the plane went to school with me.'

His hand covered hers warmly. He leaned his head back and closed his eyes. He looked exhausted, she thought tenderly, she wouldn't ask him any more questions. There was only one that really mattered, anyway.

Later dinner was served and it was fun to eat together and drink more champagne. Later still a film was shown; without wearing the ear-set it was just a sequence of flickering shadows to Kate, who was living in a dream world herself by this time.

Paul slept for a time and wakened with a jerk, turning to her with a startled look that changed to contentment. 'You're still there,' he murmured. 'Don't ever go away.' He added drowsily, 'Will your father marry us, do you think?'

Kate smiled secretly, thinking that Father would approve of Paul. He always said he liked a man to be a man, and nobody could fault Paul Caister on that score. 'I imagine I can persuade him,' she smiled.

Then she had to ask her question. 'Did you love her—Gabrielle?'

'As I said,' he grinned, 'she was prettily packaged.'

'But you must have loved her, you wanted to marry her.' She blinked. 'I suppose I shouldn't ask you that.'

'I'll allow you to—just this once. After that my past is a closed book. The fact is that it took a small grey mouse to get the message through about what love is all about.' His arm went round her, drawing her as near as their separate seats allowed. 'If I'd married Gabrielle it would have lasted about——' he looked up at the roof of the plane '—about six months.'

'And if you marry me?'

'*When* I marry you,' he corrected, 'it will last about sixty years, I reckon.'

'Sixty years is a long time.'

He leaned over so that his mouth was against

her cheek. 'We've a lot to do in between. A lot of work, a lot of fun.' His voice dropped as he added huskily, 'An awful lot of loving.'

Kate closed her eyes. She felt secure and warm and blissfully happy. One by one the reading lights over the seats went out until there was only a dim glow illuminating the compartment.

'It's going to be a long night,' Paul said softly as they tipped back their seats and covered their knees with the soft rugs provided. 'We follow the darkness going this way.' He leaned towards her and kissed her tenderly. 'Goodnight, my love.'

The great plane throbbed steadily onward under the stars, and after a time they slept, hand in hand and side by side.

What readers say about Harlequin romance fiction...

"You're #1."

A.H.,* Hattiesburg, Missouri

"Thank you for the many hours of lovely enjoyment you have given me."

M.M., Schaumburg, Illinois

"The books are so good that I have to read them all the way through before being able to go to sleep at night."

N.Q., Newark, California

"Thanks for many happy hours."

M.L., Millville, New Jersey

"Harlequin books are the doorway to pleasure."

"They are quality books—down-to-earth reading! Don't ever quit!"

"A pleasant escape from the pressures of this world."

"Keep them coming! They are still the best books."

*Names available on request

Harlequin Romances

The books that let you escape
into the wonderful world of romance!
Trips to exotic places…interesting
plots…meeting memorable people…
the excitement of love….These are
integral parts of Harlequin Romances—
the heartwarming novels read by
women everywhere.

Many early issues are now available.
Choose from this great selection!

Choose from this list of Harlequin Romance editions.*

*Some of these book were originally published under different titles.

Relive a great love story...
with Harlequin Romances
Complete and mail this coupon today!

Harlequin Reader Service

In the U.S.A.
1440 South Priest Drive
Tempe, AZ 85281

In Canada
649 Ontario Street
Stratford, Ontario N5A 6W2

Please send me the following Harlequin Romance novels. I am enclosing my check or money order for $1.25 for each novel ordered, plus 75¢ to cover postage and handling.

☐ 422	☐ 509	☐ 636	☐ 729	☐ 810	☐ 902
☐ 434	☐ 517	☐ 673	☐ 737	☐ 815	☐ 903
☐ 459	☐ 535	☐ 683	☐ 746	☐ 838	☐ 909
☐ 481	☐ 559	☐ 684	☐ 748	☐ 872	☐ 920
☐ 492	☐ 583	☐ 713	☐ 798	☐ 878	☐ 927
☐ 508	☐ 634	☐ 714	☐ 799	☐ 888	☐ 941

Number of novels checked @ $1.25 each = $_____

N.Y. and Ariz. residents add appropriate sales tax. $_____

Postage and handling $_____.75

TOTAL $_____

I enclose _____
(Please send check or money order. We cannot be responsible for cash sent through the mail.)

Prices subject to change without notice.

NAME _____
(Please Print)

ADDRESS _____

CITY _____

STATE/PROV. _____

ZIP/POSTAL CODE _____
Offer expires February 28, 1982

106563371